# The Case of the Butterscotch Burglars

## A GOSSIP COZY MYSTERY BOOK 4

ROSIE A. POINT

The Case of the Butterscotch Burglars
A Gossip Cozy Mystery Book 4

**Cover by Mariah Sinclair | TheCoverVault.com**

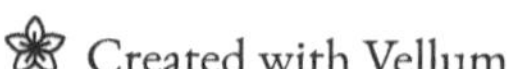 Created with Vellum

# You're invited!

Hi there, reader!

I'd like to formally invite you to join my awesome community of readers. We love to chat about cozy mysteries, cooking, and pets.

It's super fun because I get to share chapters from yet-to-be-released books, fun recipes, pictures, and do giveaways with the people who enjoy my stories the most.

So whether you're a new reader or you've been enjoying my stories for a while, you can catch up with other like-minded readers, and get lots of cool content by visiting my website at *www.rosiepointbooks.com* and signing up for my mailing list.

Or simply search for me on *www.bookbub.com* and follow me there.

I look forward to getting to know you better.

Let's get into the story!

Yours,
Rosie

# Meet the Characters

**Charlie Smith (Mission)**—An ex-spy, Charlie's lives and works in her grandmother's inn in Gossip, Texas, as a server, maid, and assistant. With her particular set of skills and spunky attitude, she's become Gossip's "fixer" thanks to her previous involvement in solving murder mysteries.

**Georgina Franklin (Mission)**—Charlie's super-spy grandmother who raised her. Georgina (or Gamma, as Charlie calls her) is the most decorated spy in the history of the NSIB. She's retired, but still as smart and spry as ever.

**Lauren Harris**—The happy-go-lucky chef at the Gossip Inn. A master baker, she's always got delicious cupcakes prepared for the inn's lunches and dinners. She's jolly, with bright red hair she wears in pigtails.

**Cocoa Puff**—Georgina's chocolate brown cat. He's friendly as can be with people he trusts. Often sleeps on Charlie's bed and accompanies her around the inn, helping her dust the various trinkets and tables.

**Sunlight**—Charlie's newly adopted cat and co-sleuth. A ginger kitty with an adventurous spirit. He loves to get up to mischief in the inn and always has Charlie's back.

**Jessie Belle-Blue**—Jessie is Georgina's worst nightmare. As the owner of the local cattery and now, a guesthouse, she hates the fact that Georgina has opened a kitten foster center in direct competition. Will do whatever it takes to come out on top.

**Detective Aaron Goode**—The new tough detective in town. He's handsome, with dark hair, a strong jawline, and unflinching determination to get to the bottom of things. He doesn't appreciate interference.

**Lisa Crocker**—The owner of the local Butterscotch Boutique. She hires Charlie to help her fix a problem she's got. A rash of break-ins where thieves are damaging her surveillance equipment and stealing the clothes and jewelry from her store!

**Barney Crocker**—Lisa's husband. A retired stockbroker who has recently returned to Gossip to enjoy his retirement with his lovely wife and his supportive mother. He wants a child but Lisa is too busy with business to focus on family.

**Grandma Crocker**—Grandma Crocker is Barney's mother, but everybody calls her Grandma because she's got plenty of grandkids from Barney's brothers and sisters. She's a real nice lady who is very, very wealthy.

**Matthew Fellers**—Lisa's cousin who is struggling financially and works at the local convenience store. Nice guy and popular with a lot of the younger crowd in Gossip.

# One

"I DON'T UNDERSTAND who would want to do this. It's unfathomable. Unbelievable. The worst thing that's happened to me in my entire life." Lisa Crocker, the owner of the Butterscotch Boutique, stood beside the glass counter in her store, her hand clutching the string of pearls at her throat. "The monsters!"

I had my notepad out, along with my stubby pencil. It wasn't exactly professional, but I'd grown accustomed to taking notes on the fly like this at the Gossip Inn. Besides, I didn't have my grandmother listening in on this conversation today.

"I understand this has to be very upsetting for you, Miss Crocker," I replied, glancing around the store.

The interior had been trashed, most of the expensive, designer wear had been stolen, including jewelry that had been kept in the glass cases near the back. The store itself had a French vibe to it. Wooden floors and curling, gold ornamentation with standing mirrors.

"It's Mrs. Crocker," Lisa replied, running fingers through her curly, yellow hair. She was skinny as a rake and wore a lace frilled blouse with a pair of high waisted slacks. I wasn't sure if that was fashionable or not, but it had to be if she was wearing it.

The Butterscotch Boutique had grown a name in Gossip. The most exclusive place to buy overpriced clothing that no one in town cared about.

That was the funny thing about clothes. Nobody cared. *Take it from a woman who wore black dresses covered in frolicking cat pictures for six months.* As long as you had enough clothes covering your body and they weren't full of holes, most people in Gossip didn't give two hoots about "who you were wearing."

I took a turn around the store, frowning at the carnage. "Did you call the police, Mrs. Crocker?"

"I did," she replied. "But they were useless! They came by which was a help for insurance purposes, but they didn't make any promises. Apparently, this isn't a *big deal* or whatever it is they said. Detective Goode has bigger cases to worry about."

"Bigger cases?"

"I don't know what he could *possibly* be investigating when nothing else has happened in town."

And I had to agree with her on that. Detective Goode was up to something, but I didn't have time to ponder what it was.

It was nearly Thanksgiving, and after a month of nothing to do, constant wondering whether I actually belonged in Gossip, and the inexorable grind of herding guests and cats at the Gossip Inn, I was in desperate need of a distraction.

Working out who had robbed the Butterscotch Boutique would have to be my new case. But I needed more information before I officially agreed. And I'd have to tell Mrs. Crocker my fee.

"So, talk me through what happened here," I said, making notes on my pad as I picked my way across the glazed wooden floor.

*Some clothes were taken but not all. A lot of clothing ripped. Why? Revenge? Or just a sloppy thief? But thieves want to keep their merchandise intact for resale.*

*All the jewelry is gone. Glass cases broken.*

I glanced up at the corners of the ceiling and frowned.

"I don't know what to say," Lisa replied. "I came in this morning and this place was a total mess. The front door was wide open, as if someone unlocked it and just came in. But that's impossible because I'm the only one who has a key."

"You don't have any assistants? Cashiers?"

"No," Lisa said. "It's just me. I'm a small business owner."

Who did everything? I made a note of that. "So you don't have an alarm system?" I asked.

"No. I was about to get one installed, but it was never a priority for me," Lisa replied. "I mean, this is Gossip. It's not like we're in the big city and crime is rife."

*Although, in retrospect, Mrs. Crocker might have to change her opinion.* "Right. But you have cameras." I pointed with the end of my stubby pencil to the corners of the ceiling. "Are they dummy cameras?"

"No, those are real. Just in case of shoplifters," Mrs. Crocker replied, sweeping over, her high heels clacking on the wooden floor. "You know, we get teens in here who dare each other to steal things. That's why I've started locking the jewelry away."

"OK. And did the police take a look at that surveillance footage or take it with them?" I asked.

"They looked at it, but there was no use. The thief erased the footage."

"They erased it?"

"Yes," Mrs. Crocker said. "They got into the office in

the back and got into my computer. I don't have a pass-word on it."

"I see."

*Not exactly security conscious.* I made that note too.

"Do you know of anyone in town who might want to target you?" I asked.

"Target me?" Lisa frowned. "No. I don't know why that would be the case. This is a robbery. They clearly wanted to resell my goods."

"Sure. That would seem to be the case," I replied, "but look at this." I bent and lifted one of the garments off the floor—a silken garment that had been ripped nearly in two.

Lisa stiffened. "What about it?"

"A thief who wants to resell goods doesn't usually damage the goods he wants to resell," I replied. "This could've been revenge." Or there was another motive I wasn't seeing. "So, is there anyone who you may have argued with recently? Or perhaps an enemy boutique?" That kind of stuff happened a lot in Gossip.

Even my grandmother, Gamma, as I called her, had an arch-nemesis. Small towns bred cozy atmospheres, friends and enemies for life. It was kind of fun, honestly.

"I don't make a habit of arguing with people," Lisa said, sniffily. "I have my little group of friends, ladies I have tea with once or twice a week, my husband, and that's about it. I like a peaceful life, Miss Smith."

"I understand. I have to check, you know, just to cover every possibility."

"I appreciate you being thorough," Lisa said, after a beat. "You've been more helpful than the police, that's for sure."

I considered the facts in the case then smiled at Mrs. Crocker. "OK," I said, "I'll take the case."

Lisa heaved a sigh of relief. "Oh, thank you. Thank goodness. If I can't trust the police to help me, then at least I'll have you. You came highly recommended, you know, Mrs. Rogers told me you helped her a great deal with the unfortunate passing of her daughter."

I bowed my head for a second, thinking about it. The past had to remain in the past, however. A hard lesson I was slowly learning thanks to my grandmother's sage advice.

"If there's anything you can tell me about what happened here, please call me." I whipped out my card— newly printed with my name and title "the Gossip Fixer" —and handed it to her. "And don't share that card with anyone, please. Especially not law enforcement." What I did wasn't illegal, but I didn't need Goode on my case.

"You have my word," Lisa said. "And if you have any questions, day or night, don't hesitate to call me." She brought out her card and gave it over. "Or if I'm unreachable by that number, you can come to my house." Mrs. Crocker produced a pen, took the card back and hastily scribbled her address down on the back. She lived on Swan Lane—a street in an affluent neighborhood.

"I will," I replied. "You know what my fees are."

"I've already sent over the first half."

I snapped a few pictures of the interior of the store then said goodbye to my client. Burglaries weren't my usual case, but it would be a fun addition to this month. There was a lot going on. Gamma's surprise birthday party was around the corner, and then there was Thanksgiving, and the cats in the—

I stepped out onto the sidewalk and bumped into a passerby. The man, wearing a gold chain and an open-necked shirt, spun toward me. "Hey, watch it!" A thick, Brooklyn accent. "Loser." He stalked off, the sun glistening on the gel in his slicked back hair.

I opened my mouth to accost him verbally then thought better of it. Charlotte Smith, the assistant at her grandmother's inn, wouldn't say boo to a goose. But Charlotte Mission, ex-spy extraordinaire—kind of— would have loved to kick him right in the heiney.

*Let it go.* I headed off with a shrug, looking forward to an afternoon of planning my grandmother's birthday party, made exciting by the fact that Gamma was an ex-spy herself, hated secrets, and might cotton on to the surprise bash at any moment.

Nobody could accuse Gossip of being boring, at least not long-term. But hey, I'd take boring over a murder, any day.

# Two

"HAVE YOU THOUGHT ABOUT IT?" Lauren, the chef at the Gossip Inn, stood beside the worn wooden table in the kitchen, rocking her baby, Rebecca, in her arms. The little angel, only a few months old, snoozed peacefully, but the minute Lauren stopped rocking, all heck would break loose. Who knew babies could be so fussy?

*Add that to the list of why I shouldn't have children.*

"Thought about what?" I asked.

"Your date."

I groaned inwardly.

Ever since Detective Goode had asked me out a month ago, and Gamma had found out about it, because she was a spy and found out just about everything that went on in the Gossip Inn, life had been complicated. I couldn't go one day without Lauren encouraging me to give it a shot or Gamma expressly forbidding it.

My grandmother oscillated between wanting me to get out of my shell and date and banning me from going near Detective Goode because he was too much like us.

It was mighty confusing. And so not what I wanted to talk about. Ever.

"Anyway," I said, and sat down at the kitchen table. "We should talk about more important matters."

"Nothing is more important than love." Lauren smiled at her baby, pausing the rocking from side-to-side. Rebecca made a tiny mewling noise that I'd come to associate with a bomb siren, and Lauren pulled a face and immediately began rocking again.

"Love and babies?"

"Don't you start with me, Charlie," Lauren said. "You know I'm happy with my little family."

I shrugged. "It's coming soon," I said, glancing over my shoulder at the archway that led from the kitchen out into the hallway beyond. The three cats who frequented the main portion of the inn, Sunlight, my adopted ginger troublemaker, Cocoa Puff, the lazy chocolate brown sweetheart, and Snowy, the newest playful addition, lay there watching us. "We've got to be careful. Be quick. Quiet."

"You mean..."

"Project Number Unknown." We'd named our secret

plan for Gamma's birthday bash under the greatest secret. Number Unknown was a nod to the fact that we wouldn't be putting sixty-nine candles on her cake, mostly because she didn't like thinking about the fact that she was sixty-nine.

*"Age is just a number, Charlotte. As is the amount of evil men I've imprisoned and killed."* Gamma's voice echoed in my mind.

"Where is our mark?" I asked Lauren.

Lauren rocked a little more nervously. "She's doing reconnaissance at Jessie Belle-Blue's guesthouse. She shouldn't be back for another hour."

"Good," I replied. "Then let's get serious. We've got the date, but what about gifts?"

"I've been thinking about that a lot," Lauren said, "and I think I might have an idea. You know how Georgina loves all her side projects?"

"Sure." My grandmother's side-projects had included the secret armory underneath the inn, the kitten foster center, and the new cat hotel for guests. Heavens, it included the Gossip Inn itself.

"I've been thinking that maybe we should get—"

Footsteps sounded in the hall, and Sunlight rose to his paws, arching his back and stretching out then disappearing from view. The curt steps, businesslike, quick, were recognizable immediately.

"So, what are we doing for lunch today?" I asked, immediately.

"Lunch?" Lauren colored. "Uh, oh, uh... eh..."

Lauren, the only person in the entirety of Gossip who knew that my grandmother and I were ex-spies, was still getting used to operating on the sly. "We don't have that many guests at this time of the year," I said, encouraging Lauren to calm down with the tiniest of gestures. "So, I guess we don't have to make that much food for lunch?"

"Yes, we only have Mr. Briggs and Miss Larson for the next week. They'll be leaving for Thanksgiving," Lauren said, her shoulders easing, but her cheeks still red as she rocked little Rebecca.

"Add another guest to the list." My grandmother entered the kitchen, wearing a neat cardigan and sling-back heels. She was flanked by a tall, meaty man with a smiley face tattooed under one eye. Quinton, relative of Jessie Belle-Blue, the current gardener at the inn who usually stayed out in the shack to avoid scaring the guests. He had... an interesting back story, and I definitely didn't trust him. Not because he'd once been accused of murder, but because of his relation to my grandmother's arch-nemesis.

"Quinton?" I raised an eyebrow.

His dog pattered up behind him, but didn't enter the kitchen. Lauren's rules were simple. No animals in the kitchen and no food fights. Oh, and no complaining about her food. Also, never touch her recipe book. And then there was the—

"Are you all right, Lauren?" Gamma asked. "Your cheeks are flushed."

"Hormones," Lauren muttered, and cast her gaze downward toward her baby.

Gamma frowned at her for a little too long, and I cleared my throat. "Quinton's going to be staying in the inn, Georgina?"

"Why, yes, he is. He's requested a room for himself and Charlie."

I grimaced. I wasn't exactly the biggest fan of the fact that Quinton's dog's name happened to be Charlie. He was a beautiful husky and a treat to have around, but every time Quinton called him, with a happy patting on his knees or thighs, it was... kind of degrading for me.

"He'll be staying on the top floor next to you, Charlotte," Gamma continued. "And he'll be taking meals with the guests. It's Thanksgiving. Why not share a little of the joy."

"Any reason why you've requested to stay in the inn?" I asked Quinton, narrowing my eyes.

I didn't want to be mean or anything, but it was hard to trust a Belle-Blue.

"Just nice in here, isn't it?" Quinton shrugged.

"And it's not as if the guests will be alarmed by his

presence," Gamma said. "Quite frankly, I was never concerned about that. It was Belle-Blue who had the problem. Not you, Quinton, your... aunt."

He nodded.

"I'm fine with it," I said. "As long as your dog doesn't make too much noise."

"Charlie's a good boy." Quinton patted Charlie on the head.

I tried not to react, but it was difficult.

"Aren't you, Charlie? Such a good boy. Yes, you are. Yes, you are. Little cutie, good boy. You wanna play fetch, huh?" The baby noises were too much to handle, so I got up and made for the exit.

"Georgina," I said, on my way past her, "would you mind coming with me? I'd like to talk to you about something."

"But of course, Charlotte. I always have time for my employees." No one knew we were related, except for Lauren, and we'd keep it that way, both for Gamma's safety and for mine.

I headed for the door to the kitten foster center. I could always use my grandmother's help on a case, and talking to her would give Lauren time to relax after we'd almost got caught planning Project Number Unknown.

Besides, this case was... intriguing. There was almost

no evidence, and I got the feeling that Lisa Crocker, my new client, hadn't exactly been forthcoming.

It was my experience that everybody in Gossip had something to hide. And my grandmother always knew their secrets.

# Three

Oddly enough, a room full of frolicking kittens, meowing, purring, and bumping up against my legs for attention, was the perfect place to contemplate cases. I found that stroking kitty fur helped power the deductive reasoning part of my brain.

I sat down on the wooden floor in the kitten foster center and stroked a black kitten who was one of the most recent additions to the center. Cinderella, as we called her, had been found under someone's porch after having been abandoned by her momma.

The poor little thing had needed to be nursed to full health before joining the older cats in this section of the center.

I stroked her, enjoying the purrs and the occasional rough-tongued lick, my eyes narrowed as I thought about the Butterscotch Boutique.

"What's on your mind, Charlotte?" Gamma glanced toward the side room where the smaller cats were kept in an incubator. The assistant watching over them, Jemimah, was engrossed in reading the local newspaper.

"I was asked by Lisa Crocker to help her solve a little problem she's having." I explained it to Gamma in brief.

"Ah," Gamma said, walking to one of the windows that looked out on the inn's sweeping grounds. "Ah, now that is interesting. A robbery in Gossip? And you say the police aren't interested?" My grandmother's British accent always reminded me of Helen Mirren playing the Queen.

"That's what Mrs. Crocker says."

"Is that so? Well, well, well."

"What is it, Georgina?"

"Mrs. Crocker doesn't have a particularly clean slate when it comes to lying," Gamma replied, turning to me again, her heels tapping on the boards. "You see, there are *rumors* that she's been having an affair."

"Would you say these rumors are unfounded?" My grandmother had an actual database containing the names, pictures, background info, and extraneous details of nearly every individual who lived in Gossip. She spent a significant amount of time curating and updating it. Another of her pet side projects.

"No, I would not. But they aren't proven, so to speak.

You see, the Crocker family has an interesting dynamic, as I recall. A husband who is well-off, a wife who has been left alone for vast periods of time. There's more to it than that, but I would need to ensure that my information is correct." Meaning she had to check her database to make sure.

"What do you know with certainty?" I asked.

"That Mr. Crocker recently retired from his high-powered career," Gamma replied, "meaning he's returned to Gossip and is spending a lot more time with his wife. My little birds tell me that he doesn't approve of his wife's business."

"The Boutique?" I asked.

"Exactly."

That was interesting. "Maybe I'll head over to Mrs. Crocker's house later on tonight," I said. "She mentioned I could stop by with questions any time. Interviewing Mr. Crocker would be helpful no matter what information he has about the boutique."

"That might be wise," Gamma replied.

"Are y'all talking about the Butterscotch Boutique?" The voice came from the half-door that separated the main portion of the center from the incubation room.

I stiffened, but Gamma's attitude didn't change. She'd known that Jemimah, her assistant, had overheard our conversation and wasn't alarmed by that.

My grandmother was the most decorated spy in the history of our agency, the NSIB, so it was no wonder she'd noticed Jemimah listening in.

"We are, indeed, Jemimah," Gamma said. "How are you today?"

"Oh, I'm fine, thank you. How are you?" Jemimah was a sweetheart, and had been with us for a few months now. Usually, we had a high turnover when it came to assistants because working at the foster center was a tough job. Late nights looking after kittens who needed feeding or constant attention because they were young and helpless, and then there was the cat hotel portion of the center where guests could drop off their full-grown cats.

"It's all coming up roses," Gamma replied. "Except for at the Butterscotch Boutique. You heard about the robbery, I assume?"

Jemimah nodded, her bright green eyes lighting up. "Oh, you bet your apron, I did." Everyone in Gossip, Texas, loved to gossip. It wasn't even a witty pun at this point, just a fact of life. "I heard that Lisa Crocker screamed blue murder for a full half an hour after she found out somebody broke in. You know how she is." Jemimah rolled her eyes.

"What do you mean by that?" I asked.

Jemimah twirled a finger through her luscious raven hair. "She's used to getting what she wants. That's what happens when you're, you know, married to one of the richest men in Gossip. I've heard stories about her."

"What kind of stories?"

"That she throws tantrums when she doesn't get what she wants. Like a toddler. People have been wondering when Barney will divorce her for years. He's been fixing to do that, according to the rumor mill."

"But he hasn't?" I asked.

"No, but he's back in Gossip now, so it's only a matter of time," Jemimah said. "You know, he's never like that Butterscotch Boutique of hers, even though he helped fund it. I don't blame him. Seems like kind of a waste of time and money in this town."

I stroked Cinderella, and she rolled over in my lap, demanding kitty belly play time. I scratched her furry belly and she clawed my hand, then lifted my hand and she opened her paws, showing me her pink toe beans.

"And you know what else?"

"What?" Gamma and I asked, in unison.

"That Butterscotch Boutique is a rip-off," Jemimah said. "I bought a cocktail dress from that place once and the zipper ripped the first time I put it on. Idiot that I am, I'd already taken off that tag so I couldn't return it."

"Bad quality?" I asked.

"Exactly. Bad quality. And it's supposed to be a designer store. I bet it was one of Lisa's disgruntled customers who broke in and stole all that stuff, just to get back at her."

It wasn't a bad deduction on her part. "Jemma," I said, "do you still have that dress?"

"I sure do."

"Would you mind bringing it in when you have your next shift so I could take a look at it?"

"Sure! I'll have to root around in my closet for it, but no problem!"

An interesting lead. It seemed there might be more to this burglary than met the eye.

Four

That evening...

I'D SPENT the rest of the afternoon helping Lauren with the lunch service—delicious roast beef, crispy potatoes, gravy, a medley of fall vegetables, and for dessert, the lemon chiffon cupcakes Lauren had been practicing for Gamma's birthday party.

Both our current guests, Mr. Briggs and Mrs. Larson, had decided to go out and eat at the Hungry Steer for dinner, so Lauren and Gamma had agreed we could cancel the dinner service.

That, in turn, had freed up some time for me to question my leads. Mr. and Mrs. Crocker.

I cruised down Gossip's Main Street in Gamma's sea-green Mini-Cooper, a smile on my lips as I passed beneath the Thanksgiving banner that had been strung up between two of the town's wrought-iron lampposts.

Folks in Gossip loved their holidays. They celebrated everything from Valentine's Day to Christmas and all the holidays in between. Heavens, they'd even created a few of their own as an excuse to keep things busy and bustling.

Ten minutes later, I entered Swan Lane—a broad street that was flanked by opulent homes tucked behind brick walls covered in plants that had already lost their leaves.

*Probably looks amazing during spring.*

Every house was a double story at the very least, and a lot of the homes had fountains or hedges cut into shapes in the front yard. What was it with wealthy folks and cutting bushes into shapes? Then again, we had some strange shaped bushes at the Gossip Inn, so who was I to judge?

An easy dusk had settled on the gates and houses, and I was tempted to open the Mini-Cooper windows to allow some of the fresh fall air into the car, but it was nippier than usual tonight, even for Texas.

"Now, where are you?" I slowed, searching the houses for numbers.

The flashing of red and blue lights up ahead drew my focus, and I pulled over right away. What was this?

I emerged from the Mini-Cooper and instantly regretted it.

Detective Goode, my tormentor both because he was incredibly handsome and overbearing, and because he disapproved of my interfering nature, stood nearby, talking under his breath with a police officer.

I froze.

There were two options: keep standing here until he saw me or slink back into the Mini and try to high-tail it out of here.

I shifted, hoping to dart back into the car, but Goode instantly looked over at me and raised an eyebrow. The man was like a T-Rex from *Jurassic Park*, attracted to movement.

*Darn it.*

I glanced up at the house and reconsidered my irritation. The police cars were parked outside the Crocker household! And Mrs. Crocker and an elderly woman stood outside the gates, talking to two police officers.

Was my client in danger?

*Careful, Charlie, you don't want to get on Goode's bad side this time.*

How dare Goode try to stop me from protecting the people of this town? How dare he usurp the only real good I could do for—?

"Miss Smith," Goode said, swaggering over in his usual

arrogant manner. He tucked his fingers into the belt loops of his jeans and tilted his head to one side. "Fancy meeting you here."

"Fancy? There's nothing fancy about it. I'd say this is the furthest from 'fancy' I've ever been."

"What's the matter, Smith, woke up on the wrong side of the bed this morning?"

"It's eight at night," I replied, waspishly.

"You strike me as one of those women."

I huffed.

Goode chuckled. "Easy. I mean, one of those people."

"And what type of person is that, exactly?" Why, oh why, did this guy get under my skin like this? It had nothing to do with his perfectly parted black hair or his penetrating green eyes, or even how good his lemony cologne smelled. Of course not. It was because he was an arrogant, know-it-all, detective who—

"The type of person who lets one bad morning affect the rest of their day."

"Aren't you delightful?"

"We established that the last time we talked," he said. "Remember? When I asked you out for coffee and you never called me back?"

*Do. Not. Blush.* "Anyway," I said, "what's going on? I have an appointment with Mrs. Crocker."

"An appointment?"

*Shoot. Don't be so professional. He's not supposed to know.* "I mean, she's my friend. I'm supposed to be having dinner with her."

"At this time?"

"What's the matter, Goode? Are you getting to the age where your digestive system has ceased to function after a certain time of night."

"That's mighty ageist of you."

I clammed my lips together. Shoot. I hated it when he was right. "That's not what I meant."

He gave me one of those sparkling grins. "I'm sure Georgina would love to hear your thoughts on age."

"I have the same thoughts as she does. That it doesn't matter." It had been a stupid thing to do, taunting him about age, but he brought out the *stupidity* in me quite easily. I took a breath and calmed myself. "Anyway, what's going on? Is Mrs. Crocker all right?"

"She's fine," Goode replied. "It's Mr. Crocker that's not so hot."

"Why?"

Goode's gaze traveled over me, from head to toe, and I tried not to react. Why did the man simultaneously irritate me and give me shivers?

*Because you like him?* "What?" I challenged him.

"I don't want you getting involved."

"Since when have I ever gotten involved in your cases?"

Many times, but he couldn't prove it and that was the point.

"Mr. Crocker's been murdered," Detective Goode said, at last. "You wouldn't happen to know anything about that, would you?"

"I literally just got here. Call Georgina if you don't believe me. Or Lauren Harris."

"Relax, Smith, I wasn't accusing you of murder. Merely suggesting you might have information."

I licked my lips and glanced at Mrs. Crocker and the older woman next to her. "I don't know anything." *Unfortunately.*

I hated to say it. But I wouldn't allow my lack of information to last for long. Mr. Crocker had been murdered right after the Butterscotch Boutique had been burgled? When Mr. Crocker hadn't approved of his wife's owning the store.

This case was about to get a lot more complicated.

"You don't know anything," Detective Goode said, scanning me again. "Good. Keep it that way." He sauntered across the road without so much as a goodbye.

*Five*

*The following morning...*

NATURALLY, I hadn't been able to hang around and wait for information while Detective Goode was there, watching like a hawk. But returning to the literal scene of the crime the next day was fine by me.

I parked my grandmother's sea-green Mini-Cooper outside the Crocker residence on Swan Lane, the sunlight bright, the sky cloudless today. Compared to yesterday, it was mild, but there was still a chill to the breeze as I emerged into the fall morning.

The house was silent, at least from the outside, and there were no cop cars in sight.

Last night, I hadn't managed to ascertain where Mr. Crocker had died. Inside the house? Outside? In the yard? And the how was an equal mystery, though Gamma had set to work trying to find out the minute she'd heard about the murder. No luck yet.

I checked the street both ways before crossing and hitting the buzzer on the intercom at the gate.

A minute passed, and I pressed it again.

"Hello?" An older woman's voice, crackling a little. "Who is it?"

"Hi there," I said, and fluffed my short blonde hair, hoping they didn't have cameras. Nobody looked good through the viewpoint of a fish-eye lens. Gamma theorized that it was easy to look like a criminal through one. "My name is Charlotte Smith. I'm here to see Mrs. Crocker."

A silence.

"Hello?"

"Yes, yes, I hear you. Lisa is around here *somewhere*, but this is quite a bad time, you know. A terrible time even."

"I'm sorry," I said, "I heard about... your loss."

"Yes, thank you. I suppose I should let you in. No doubt Lisa will be annoyed with me if I don't." The gates clicked and swung inward, and I walked up the long pathway toward the house. White-walled, imposing, with thick curtains in the windows, and a cat sunning itself on the front porch.

That was a good sign. I generally liked cat people. But of course, it depended on who owned the cat.

I mounted the steps and the doors opened. The older lady came out. "Charlotte, you said?"

"Yes," I replied, and extended a hand. "It's nice to meet you."

"I believe Lisa mentioned something about a Charlotte. Something regarding that ridiculous shop of hers."

"I'm helping her figure out who broke into the Butterscotch Boutique."

"Yes, that was what I meant. I'm Grandma Crocker. Not my first name, but that's what my grandchildren call me, so that's what I prefer." She had a strong grip and gave my finger an extra squeeze before letting go. "You really think you can figure that out? The robbery and so on?"

"That's what I do," I replied.

Grandma Crocker narrowed her eyes at me and lifted one gnarled finger. She bobbled it in the air. "Wait a second," she said. "I know who you are. You're Georgina Franklin's assistant at the Gossip Inn."

"Yeah, I am. Are you friends with Georgina?"

"Oh, we have our moments. Little troublemaker that Georgina." Grandma Crocker gave a fond smile. "But yes, I have heard about you. What is it they call you?"

"The Gossip Fixer," I said, and with no small measure of pride. I had wanted to fit in with the town for so long, to find my place, to be satisfied with small town living.

"Now, that's interesting. What does it take to become a fixer?"

"It's kind of like being a private investigator except more active, and a little more dangerous sometimes," I said.

"Dangerous." Grandma Crocker looked thoughtful, and for a woman who had just lost her son, not all that sad.

"What's going on out here?" Lisa appeared in the doorway. The cat on the porch got up and streaked off. *Bad sign if ever I saw one.*

"Do you have to do that, Lisa? You scared Mitzy."

Lisa ignored Grandma Crocker and exited onto the porch. "Miss Smith. I'm glad you're here, but I'm afraid this is a terrible time."

"I heard," I said. "I'm so sorry for your loss. I came by last night, actually. I wanted to talk to you and your... well, your family."

"Oh," Lisa sighed. "Oh yeah." She gave an exaggerated sniff and withdrew a Kleenex from the pocket of her jeans. She dabbed it underneath either eye.

All the while, Grandma Crocker observed her with a

great deal of skepticism. "I was just thinking that I'll hire Miss Smith here to find out what happened to my son."

Lisa had been in the process of dabbing her nose. She inhaled so sharply half the Kleenex disappeared up her left nostril. Lisa choked and snorted. "W-what? That's not a good idea."

"Why not," Grandma Crocker asked. "If she's smart enough to figure out who broke into your store, then surely she can help me with this. Have you got any experience with murder investigations, Miss Smith?"

"This is wrong," Lisa said. "Dora, you should let the police handle this."

"Like you let the police handle your problem?" Grandma Crocker countered.

The women glared at each other, neither puffy-eyed, nor seeming that distraught over Mr. Crocker's death. I understood that grief took different forms but this was... *odd*.

"I've handled murder investigations, yes," I said. "But I prefer to keep that information within a small circle of friends and clients."

"Excellent," Grandma Crocker replied. "I'd like you to figure out who murdered my Barney, and why. And then I want you to make them pay."

"Pay," I said.

"Oh yes. Pay. I want you to find the woman and hunt her down."

"Woman?" That came from me and Lisa.

I wasn't used to talking in unison with anyone other than my grandmother, and I gave Lisa a disconcerted look.

"I saw who did it," Grandma Crocker said.

"Just a minute, Grandma." I brought my notepad and stubby pencil out. "Can you tell me exactly what happened?"

"You're supposed to be here about my case," Lisa said. "Not this."

"The two incidents might be connected." I tapped the pencil nib on my page. "What are the chances that your boutique would be robbed and this would happen to Mr. Crocker all within 24 hours."

"Excellent point, Miss Smith. I like you already."

"Please, walk me through what happened," I said.

So, Grandma Crocker launched into the tale while Lisa retreated to the porch swing and sat down, her arms folded, and a small piece of tissue still stuck to the left side of her nose.

"Barney and I wanted to go for dinner, and Lisa said she would tag along," Grandma started.

"No, Barney and I were going for dinner, and you said you wanted to come with us," Lisa interjected.

Grandma Crocker waved away the complaint. "Barney, Lisa and I were on our way out. We were in Barney's Audi when he realized he had forgotten his wallet. My Barney liked to treat me, you see, so he got out of the car to run up to the house and get it. And that was when it happened." Grandma Crocker's bottom lip trembled. "There was a gunshot. It came from the bushes on the other side of the street."

Lisa nodded in agreement to that fact.

"I looked over," Grandma Crocker continued, "and that was when I saw her. A woman about this tall." She gestured above her head and just below mine. "She had hair as red as a tomato, that was why I noticed her, and she took off running toward one of the houses on the opposite side of the road. She leaped over a wall and disappeared."

"Did you see this woman?" I asked Lisa.

"No. I didn't see a red-haired woman. I saw a man."

"What?" This time, it was from me and Grandma Crocker. I didn't like this talking in unison with strangers thing one bit.

"No offense, Dora, but it sounds like you're seeing things. I saw a guy wearing a hoodie and trainers running off down the street. He went that way." She gestured in the opposite direction to the one Grandma Crocker had indicated.

"I see." I wrote that down as well.

"You're a little liar," Grandma Crocker said.

"Excuse me? I am not a liar. You're delusional," Lisa snapped.

I observed in silence.

*Tension in the family.* I noted down. *Motive? Burglary connected to the murder?*

"Is there anything else you can tell me? Do you know of anyone who may have wanted to harm Mr. Crocker? Any enemies he might've had?"

"My Barney was an angel," Grandma Crocker said. "He didn't have any enemies."

"No. Barney was a good man. He didn't cause any trouble. Besides, he recently retired and returned home. No one in town has any reason to want to... hurt him." Another fake-sounding sniffle from Lisa.

Grandma Crocker fluffed her fluffy white hair and rolled her eyes. "What do you say, Miss Smith? Will you take the case?"

"Sure," I said. "But I do have a fee."

"I can afford to double your fee," Grandma Crocker replied.

"I haven't even told you what it is yet."

"It doesn't matter. Whatever you need, I can provide." Grandma Crocker's grin was broad. She didn't notice Lisa's hateful stare boring into the back of her head.

## Six

I EXITED ONTO THE SIDEWALK, bringing my phone out of my pocket, my mind on the possible connection between the cases. I stood by what I'd said to Lisa and Grandma Crocker. What were the chances that two events would affect their family in such rapid succession and not be connected? Slim to none.

I typed a text to Gamma.

*Meet at the rendezvous point in twenty?*

My grandmother's reply was nearly instant. *Wilco.*

I could always count on Gamma to have my back. And to be interested in what I needed to get done. It was nice having a partner in crime for stuff like this. The irony being that we were the ones trying to solve the crimes.

I approached the Mini-Cooper then paused, glancing up and down the street. Mr. Crocker had been shot in front of the gates, yes? Creepy, but good information. I aligned myself with the gates and followed the two directions I'd been given with my eyes.

Grandma Crocker had mentioned a redhead appearing out of a bush, and there was only one bush big enough to hide a person across the street.

I headed over to it, peered around it, and blinked.

*Ah-ha.* A footprint. Or rather, a shoe print from a sneaker. Not a woman's size either. So, either Grandma Crocker was lying about the redhead, though I couldn't figure out why, or the short woman in question had comically large feet or shoes.

Regardless, I snapped a picture of the shoe print before heading over to the Mini-Cooper.

Twenty minutes later, I was back at the Gossip Inn, sitting under our favorite oak tree, waiting for Gamma.

She emerged from the inn wearing a cute frilly apron and a scowl.

"Uh oh," I said. "What's the problem?"

"Lauren's hiding something from me," she replied, instantly. "Do you know what it is?"

"No." A lie, but I had lied enough during my tenure as a spy that my heart rate didn't blip. "And why on earth would Lauren hide anything from you?"

"I don't know, but I can tell she's up to something.

She keeps freezing whenever I enter a room. And she won't let me taste the cream cheese frosting."

"Weird," I replied. "I'll talk to her about it."

"I would appreciate it. I don't see another solution short of interrogation, and I'd prefer not to upset Lauren by interrogating her or using my truth serum."

"You got more of that stuff?" I asked.

"Yes. My supplier contacted me with a two-for-one deal."

"A two-for-one deal on truth serum," I replied, sardonically. "Now, I've heard everything."

"This is more shocking to you than the time we found a man living in the walls?"

"Good point."

Gamma sat down on the bench beside me and smoothed her apron over her knees. "You know, I would absolutely murder for a pumpkin-spiced latte right about now."

"Uh..."

"Oh relax," Gamma said. "I wouldn't murder an innocent. Just an arms dealer or the like."

"I find that concerning, regardless."

Gamma sighed. "You must learn to take a joke, Charlotte. It's imperative to keep one's humor while living in a small town with people like Jessie Belle-Blue."

I nodded.

"Now, what did you want to meet about? The burglary?"

"The murder," I replied, and told her everything that had occurred at the Crocker household. "And I'm pretty sure that there's got to be a connection. What are the chances that the robbery and the murder happened to the same family and it's just a coincidence?"

"I would have to call my statistics guy, Rod, to answer that," Gamma said.

"Do you have a guy for everything?"

"Everything except doing things around the inn," Gamma replied. "Interestingly, I find that most men who are asked to do things around the house will invariably say yes, then take an eternity to get around to it, then get angry when you decide to finally do that thing yourself. It's not worth the extra steps. Might as well just hang the picture oneself."

"How long have you been keeping that pent up?" I asked. "And here I was thinking you were the romantic? I thought you were crushing on the local veterinarian."

"I've moved onto greener pastures," Gamma said.

"Which pastures are those?"

"They've got two signs pegged in the moist soil outside the gates." My grandmother paused for effect. "Peace and quiet."

I snorted.

Footsteps crunched up the gravel pathway toward us, and we turned. My heart flipped in my chest, little betrayer that it was. Detective Goode approached, wearing a buttoned shirt, jeans, and his lanyard bearing his ID around his neck.

"Good morning, ladies."

"Detective Goode," Gamma nodded. "To what do we owe the distinct pleasure of your presence?"

Goode eyed her then glanced at me. "I see where you're picking up the sarcasm, now. You spend a lot of time with Miss Franklin?"

I snorted a second time then stopped myself and frowned instead. "What do you want, Goode?" I wouldn't give him the honor of laughing at his jokes, even if they were accurate.

"To take you out."

"Goodness," Gamma whispered. "Quite forward, these men nowadays."

"Yeah," I replied, "at least buy me dinner first."

"That's what I'm trying to do," Goode replied. "But you've been as slippery as an eel."

"A sure fire way to get a woman to date you," I said. "Call her an eel. My favorite animal."

Goode actually colored and scratched the back of his neck, and I hated how cute he looked. Why did he get under my skin this much?

"Charlotte," Gamma said, "I'll meet you in the spot once you're finished here." She rose from the bench and gave Goode a look that would've shriveled a plum into a prune. "Keep a civil tongue in your head with my assistant, young man." And then she was off.

"She's intimidating," Goode said.

"That's what I like about her."

An awkward silence drifted between us, punctuated only by the wind and a few leaves being swept across the lawn.

Detective Goode cleared his throat. "I'd like to take you out this weekend. For dinner. I'd like to get to know you better. I understand we have... some chemistry, but I want to see if there's anything we have in common beyond that."

"Chemistry. Is that really what you think we have?" I asked, blushing.

He kept hold of me with his deadpan stare, and I couldn't help my palms getting clammy. "Don't you?"

I let the question percolate.

"Fine," I said. "This Saturday. At 08:00 p.m. and no later. You can pick me up here."

Goode's grin was massive, and I blushed again. "See you then, Charlotte."

"Charlie," I replied. "I like Charlie better."

"Charlie." He walked off a short way before pausing and looking back. "You look pretty today."

I tried not to melt into the bench. I couldn't afford to let him distract me. There were murderers and thieves to catch!

<h1 style="text-align:center">Seven</h1>

Gamma was always the most at home when she was in front of her touchscreen desk in her underground armory. She rocked from side-to-side on her chair, tapping on the screen and humming under her breath.

I wandered between the rows of shelves containing ammunition, grenades, and other small projectiles, contemplating the case or trying to. Goode had provided a significant distraction with his question.

"What do you think I should do next?" I asked, lifting a grenade from the rack and considering it. It was oddly shaped. "Case out Lisa's boutique in case the criminals come back? Follow her? Perhaps, interview her again? I didn't get much out of her both the first and second times we talked. She was distracted by Grandma Crocker."

"I think the contradicting stories that Dora and Lisa

told are interesting," Gamma said, still tapping away. "You should look into that and the family in more depth."

"The husband might've had enemies in one of the bigger cities that followed him here. A shooting like that? It sounds more like the killer was a trained professional. This wasn't poisoning or a smothering or any of the other more personal methods of taking somebody out. He was shot in cold blood." I turned the oddly shaped thing over and lifted it. Was it ever-so-slightly translucent?

"That's a good point, Charlotte," Gamma said, without looking up from her screen. "And for heaven's sake, put that down. It's an acid grenade."

I grimaced and returned the grenade to the shelf. I knew better than to fiddle with my grandmother's

"toys" but I needed something to distract myself.

*A date. I'm going on a date?*

It seemed so serious. I wasn't used to serious, unless you counted murder investigations. I didn't need a distraction when I was still trying to figure out whether I was actually meant to stay in Gossip. I couldn't live in Gamma's inn forever. I couldn't just be an assistant forever. I couldn't just—

"As far as I can tell," Gamma said, "Barney Crocker didn't have any enemies. He was well-liked by everyone, even when he was working in Texas as a stock broker."

"That's not helpful. There has to be someone who wanted to off him."

"Indeed," Gamma replied. "The Crocker family doesn't have much to show for itself. There's a distant cousin who lives in town on Lisa's side, a Mr. Matthew Fellers. He works at the convenience store and I know he's popular with the younger crowd. Party boy. And then there's Dora, who's a battle-axe but worth knowing. Smart as a whip, rich, and funny. And then there's Lisa. For a woman who isn't that remarkable, she has quite a few skeletons in her closet. Or at least one large one."

"Oh?"

"My limited research has told me a few things about Mrs. Crocker. She's worried about what other people think of her, her mother-in-law, Dora, doesn't like her at all and never thought she was good enough for Barney, and she was having an affair."

I blinked. "An affair?"

"That's the rumor," Gamma said, beckoning for me to join her.

I peered over my grandmother's shoulder at the desk. She had an email open from one of her "grapes." The people who were a part of the vine of gossipers that got back to her with details about the lives of others in Gossip.

"Nancy seems to think she was having an affair," Gamma said, gesturing to the email. "Had been meeting with a man who was not a member of the family, frequently."

"What does he look like?" I asked, scanning the email.

"No detail on that, but an affair is a motive for murder."

"You're suggesting that Lisa might've hired a killer herself?" I asked. "Murder-for-hire? Then why the burglary?"

"To cover her tracks? No, you're right, that doesn't make sense." Gamma sighed. "That or the crimes aren't connected."

"There's something going on. Something... I just wish I could fathom what it was," I said.

"There's something else." Gamma rolled her chair back, crossing her ankles and leaning casually. "Barney Crocker was fast heading toward financial ruin. Apparently, they couldn't afford the house and were considering selling."

"Life insurance policy in Lisa's name?" I suggested.

"Perhaps. Perhaps. But I'm not sure."

I nibbled on the inside of my cheek. "Maybe it's something I can find out."

THE QUESTION WAS, how did I find out whether Lisa despised her husband and wanted to murder him for money without letting Lisa know that I wanted to find out whether she despised her husband and wanted to murder him for money?

It wasn't the easiest task I had been set, but it sure beat hunting arms dealers in foreign countries.

I took a breath as I parked the Mini outside the Butterscotch Boutique. The elegant sign in the glass front door still read "CLOSED" but there was movement inside.

Lisa was in the store. Cleaning, perhaps? Plotting Grandma Crocker's murder?

The way Grandma Crocker had acted about money, it seemed like she had a lot of it. And if Barney had had little, it stood to reason that Lisa hadn't had any either.

*No money but running an exclusive boutique. Interesting.*

I knocked on the front door.

Lisa opened it. "Oh, it's you again," she said. "What is it?"

"Mind if I come in, Mrs. Crocker? I didn't get a chance to talk to you about the break-in at the store this morning."

"I was just about to get a late lunch." Lisa shifted her weight from one foot to the other.

*This woman is hiding something.*

"Oh great," I said, reading her bluff. "I could come with you."

"No, no, I'm fine with talking here." She stepped back and allowed me into the empty boutique. The place was still a mess, but it wasn't as empty as I'd thought.

A goofy-lookin' dude stood near the racks, leaning on one of them casually, texting on his phone. He was super tall, wearing ill-fitting jeans that cut into his belly and created a muffin-top, and was sweating up a storm. It was a miracle the phone didn't slip out of his hand.

"Sorry," Lisa said. "I was just talking to Mr. Dolgner about his wife. She was looking for a dress for a wedding. Isn't that right, Mr. Dolgner."

"Yeah."

"I'm afraid I can't help you at the moment, as you can see." Lisa gestured to the mess of clothing. "You'll have to come back later."

"OK." The sweaty Dolgner shrugged and sauntered out of the store, letting the door slam shut behind him.

"He's uh... pungent," I said.

"Yeah, he's got a sweat gland issue." Lisa gestured toward her underarms. "I'll open some windows." She did exactly that, taking her sweet time.

"I'm glad I caught up with you," I said, smiling. "Like I said, I didn't get much of a chance to talk to you about the break-in."

"Right. What did you want to know?"

"Now that this terrible event with your husband has transpired," I said, "I want to examine the case in a new light. Are you sure that Barney didn't have any enemies? Anyone who might've wanted to make an example out of your store before... doing what they did last night?"

Lisa paled, her lips thinning. "An example?"

"Yes," I said. "Wealthy businessmen like your husband tend to accrue enemies." I waited.

"No, there wasn't anyone. I'm sure of it."

*She didn't dispute the fact that he was wealthy.* "May I ask you a few personal questions, Mrs. Crocker? They might help me get closer to the truth about who broke into your store. You do want justice to be served, right?"

"Yes, of course." But she trembled. Oh, how she trembled. What was with this lady?

Was she just terrible at hiding her guilt? Was it as simple as her hiring someone to murder Barney? But then why the break-in here?

"Were you and your husband on good terms?" I asked.

"Of course! I loved him dearly."

"That's good," I said, slowly. "And was Mr. Crocker in any debt? Perhaps, he had debtors who might've—"

"I don't appreciate your line of questioning," Lisa said. "I hired you to find out who robbed me, not who murdered my husband. And certainly not to pry in my private affairs."

"Your mother-in-law—"

"Is delusional!" Lisa snapped. "She has no idea what she's talking about. There was no woman there last night, and she was wrong to hire you when there are police to investigate serious crimes."

"Serious crimes like burglary."

"Well, no, that's different," she said. "They don't take burglary seriously."

"But they're taking your husband's death seriously?" I asked, pushing a little harder.

"Yes!" Lisa swallowed. "I don't have any new information about what happened here. Now, if you'll excuse me, I'd like to go to lunch." She picked up her designer purse from the glass countertop and gestured with it to the door.

"I'm sorry for upsetting you, Mrs. Crocker. I'm just trying to help."

Lisa didn't say anything as I slipped out of the door and onto the sidewalk. Surprisingly, I wasn't afraid of losing her as a client. Maybe because she looked increasingly suspicious with every passing moment.

# Eight

*That night...*

I PRESSED my finger to my lips, holding my bedroom door open, and gesturing toward the figure standing at the end of the hall. Lauren, wearing a pair of stripey cotton PJs and her hair in pigtails, crept down the hall toward me.

This wasn't a coincidental slumber party. Lauren had left the babies, Tyke and Rebecca, with her husband, Jason, who had deigned to start acting like a real man ever since his daughter's birth. All of this, so Lauren could sneak back over to the Gossip Inn.

Project Unknown Number had to proceed. With the murder and the robbery, and three meals to prepare for approximately three people everyday—Quinton Belle-Blue ate like person three, four and five—life had been too busy for secret plans.

Lauren sneaked into my bedroom, and I shut the door, quietly.

She sat down on the edge of my bed, unable to stop giggling. "I feel like I'm in high school again," she whispered.

Cocoa Puff, who lay beside my pillow, opened one eye and watched her. He purred happily at our visitor. Sunlight stretched out at the bottom of my bed and dug his claws into her pants. Snowy lay on my dressing table stool, fast asleep, white paws tucked beneath her furry body.

"It's like the kitten foster center in here," Lauren whispered, giggling again.

"They like sleeping with me." I shrugged, then pressed a finger to my mouth. I leaned against the wall, my ear to the crack between my door and wall, listening. If Gamma had any inkling that we were up to something, she'd listen in, and I had to be prepared for that. My grandmother was the sharpest tool in every shed. No, she was an arsenal of incredibly sharp tools.

Lauren waited patiently, giggling and trying to stop herself.

Finally, I nodded, satisfied that Gamma hadn't

emerged from her room, then turned to Lauren. "OK," I said, "first things first, you've got to stop freaking out."

"I'm not freaking out."

"Georgina seems to think you are. She said you're hiding something from her. You banned her from tasting the cream cheese frosting."

"Yeah, because it's got lemon zest in it. If she tastes that, she'll know for sure that I'm making her lemon chiffon cupcakes for her birthday and the surprise will be ruined."

"Well, you've got to come up with another excuse for why," I said. "Or she'll surely get more suspicious and start snooping. That's the last thing we need. If we want Project Unknown Number to go ahead without a hitch, we have to be careful."

"Right." Lauren wiped the grin from her face.

"That doesn't mean we can't have fun, though."

The smile returned. Lauren was a lovely person, and while this wasn't a critical mission, I wanted it to go off without a hitch and have her enjoy herself as well.

"OK," I whispered. "So you were telling me about an idea you had?"

"Right, so I was thinking we should create an exploration pack," Lauren replied.

"What's that?" I perched my booty on the edge of the dressing table so as not to disturb Snowy on the stool.

"So, an exploration pack is like a collection of artistic pursuits that Georgina could take up. Like we give her an easel and sketchbook with art supplies, then a typewriter for her to explore writing, as well as a guitar to learn music. You know how much she enjoys her projects, maybe she would like to explore creatively as well."

"That's an awesome idea." I clapped my hands quietly.

"You really think so?" Lauren asked.

"Of course, I do! That's amazing. Georgina will love that."

"Yay. I'm so glad you think so. I was worried you wouldn't like it."

"No way. That's great." I chewed on the inside of my cheek, glancing toward the door. "Now, we just have to plan everything else. The party, the food, that kind of stuff."

"And the guest list," Lauren said. "But I can take care of that. I know who Georgina's grapes and friends are."

"Perfect. Then let's get to planning."

Lauren whipped out her phone and made notes as we planned the minutiae of the party, food, and drink. It was a lot of fun, and we had to be conscious about keeping quiet in case my grandmother woke up and heard us.

"No candles on the cake," I whispered, as a final reminder.

"As if I could forget. Georgina would never let me live that down."

"Me neither."

I sighed, trying to relax my shoulders. Even now, during our fun chat about the birthday party, I couldn't stop worrying about my cases, Goode, and my place in Gossip. Was I meant to stay here? Did I belong? Did the people in this town need me?

And more importantly, was I happy with the life I had chosen?

They were intense questions for a Monday night.

"Charlie?" Lauren prompted. "Are you OK?"

"Mmm, I guess. Just thinking about things. The case, mainly." I wasn't that great with sharing my emotions.

"What about it?"

I liked talking to Lauren about this kind of thing. She had great contacts and, several times, had given me ideas. Though, she did have a penchant for believing in the supernatural.

Briefly, I told her about my predicament—that I had two witnesses who had seen two different things.

"A woman with red hair?" Lauren asked. "Well, it wasn't me."

I laughed. "I know that. I'm just wondering who it was."

"Tell you what," Lauren said, "I can make a list of redheads for you."

"Huh? How?"

"There aren't that many redheads in Gossip," she said, "and I happen to know most of them. Besides, we do have the Gossip Redheads United. Us folks with red hair have got to stick together."

I blinked. "I didn't know that was a thing."

"Oh, it's a thing. Gossip has lots of weird little clubs," Lauren said.

"Thanks, Laur. I appreciate the help." I wouldn't be holding out any hope, but it would be at least one lead in this rather "clue-free" case.

So far, the only suspicion I had was that it had been the wife whodunit.

# Nine



*The following morning...*

"CHARLIE! HEY, CHARLIE!" The whispered hiss came from down the hall.

"Did you hear that?" I asked Lauren and Gamma.

The chef stood in front of the stove in the kitchen, wearing her apron and holding a wooden mixing spoon. We had a breakfast service soon. My grandmother was chopping potatoes, occasionally glancing at the local newspaper, *The Gossip Rag,* that was laid out on the table in front of her.

I could barely make them out through the thick ski goggles I wore. In my hand, I clutched a knife, and several onions lay on the cutting board in front of me. The goggles were my usual preventative wear for onion-cutting.

Both of them looked up. "What?" Lauren asked.

"Charlie?" The hiss came again.

"I heard that," Gamma said, and got up from the table.

"It's a ghost!" Lauren dropped her spoon into the holder on the counter. "It's a ghost for sure."

A figure appeared in the archway before Gamma could reach it. Jemimah from the kitten foster center smiled at us. "Sorry," she said. "I didn't mean to freak you out. I just wanted to talk to Charlie."

"Hey, Jemimah," I said. "What's up?"

"You mentioned that you wanted to see the dress I bought?" Jemimah lifted a pile of silken cloth. "With the zipper that broke? From the Butterscotch Boutique."

"Yeah, I did, thank you. That's awesome. I appreciate you bringing it out here." I lifted my ski goggles onto my head and walked over.

"No problem. Look, you can keep it. It's trash." She handed the dress to me.

"Thanks. If you're sure...?"

"Absolutely." And off she went, heading to her duties in the kitten foster center.

I examined the dress, turning it over. "This is silk?"

"Let me take a look." Gamma took the dress from me. "It's cheaply made. This is not silk. It's synthetic, a mock-silk if you will, and it's not very well done either. She got this from the Butterscotch Boutique?"

"That's what she said."

"That's supposed to be a designer store," Lauren said, lifting her spoon again and returning to her cooking. "That's really strange."

Gamma and I exchanged a look, and I was almost entirely sure I knew exactly what she was thinking. It was time we took a closer look at Mrs. Crocker's activities and found out the truth. Like, why was she stocking subpar clothing in her store?

I could only think that it was financially motivated. And finances might've been the reason Mr. Crocker had been murdered.

The connection was fuzzy, but there. And my suspicions about Lisa were firming by the second.

THIS WAS one of the only times in my memory that we'd taken my grandmother's black SUV with it's tinted windows into Gossip during the day. But we had a reason for it. First, that Lisa had seen Gamma's Mini-Cooper and would be alerted if she noticed us following her, and second, it had a great air-conditioner.

OK, so there was a third reason too. Nobody knew

Gamma owned it, and we were unidentifiable because of that.

We parked down the street from the Butterscotch Boutique, watching the foot traffic moving down the paved sidewalk past the storefronts with their striped awnings. We had witnessed Lisa arrive and carry several bags out to be placed in a dumpster down the alleyway between her store and the antique store next to it.

If I hadn't known better, I would've been sure that she was carting off a body. A grim thought.

"Cleaning up," I said, as Lisa emerged a third time.

"Not this time. No bags," Gamma replied, lifting her fancy black binoculars. They were small and had a stunningly powerful zoom.

"I'm surprised you haven't managed to find contact lenses that zoom in on targets," I said.

"Oh trust me, it's not for lack of trying," Gamma replied. "They're surprisingly complex. Our mark is on the move." Gamma, who had taken multiple advanced driving courses and could evade most dangerous situations, put the car in gear.

Lisa had climbed into an Audi that I assumed was Mr. Crocker's. She drove off, and we followed, keeping a distance of two cars between her bumper and our hood.

"She might just be taking a lunch break."

"True," Gamma said. "Or she's up to something."

I hoped it was the latter. I needed a lead, any lead, in this case that didn't involve poor Lauren listing all the redheads born in Gossip.

Lisa parked her car across from a small cafe called the Gossip Bistro, a relatively new establishment, and got out. She glanced around, muttered under her breath, then headed toward it. She took a seat at one of the tables outside and kept looking around, her behavior almost frantic.

"Oh, she's up to something all right," I said.

"Very shifty," Gamma agreed.

Finally, Lisa's "date" appeared. A young man wearing sunglasses, a tank top, and cargo shorts. Tan and stringy, he slopped along like he had not a care in the world.

Lisa glared at him as he sat down.

"The affair?" I asked.

"No," Gamma said. "That, I believe, is Lisa's cousin. The one I mentioned? Matthew Fellers. All my sources said they have little to no contact."

"Then why are they having lunch together?"

# Ten

LISA LEFT the bistro before her cousin did, and Gamma
and I hung around, waiting in the car for him to leave. Lisa
wouldn't give us information, but we could certainly pry it
out of Matthew Fellers. He would never see us coming.

I unclipped my seatbelt and got into the back of
the car.

"He's on the move," Gamma said.

I readied myself, bracing myself against the seats as she
started driving. I didn't have to worry too much about the
ride being rough. Gamma's driving was as skillful as I
remembered. She followed Matthew as he strolled down
the sidewalk and took several turns.

The guy was so involved in his phone and being
relaxed that he didn't notice our SUV driving up alongside
him.

Once we'd reached a quiet street, Gamma drew the car level with our target. She mounted the curb, and only then did Matthew recognize he was in danger. He threw up his arms and tried to step back, but it was already too late.

I opened the back door, leaped out, grabbed him around the throat, and drew him into the SUV. It took all of ten seconds from the curb mounting to him being in the car.

Matthew let out a terrified yelp. I covered his mouth.

"Easy," I said. "Easy. You're not going to get hurt."

"Assuming you comply with us and don't struggle," Gamma put in.

So far, Matthew had seen nothing but sky and the interior of the SUV, but if he turned his head, he would surely see us, and possibly recognize Gamma.

My grandmother, thankfully, had thought of that. Kind of. She handed me a sleeping mask. I took it and affixed it over Matthew's eyes.

"What do you want from me?" he squeaked. "I don't have any money."

"We know that," Gamma replied. "And we don't need your money."

"Then... what do you want?"

"To talk," I replied, holding him tight, my bicep cutting into his throat. "You lie, and I'll make you regret it." I tightened my grip.

Gamma grinned at me. We both knew that we weren't going to do anything to Mr. Fellers, but he had no idea. Poor guy.

I released the tighter grip.

"What do you want to know?" he gasped. "I'll tell you anything."

"What were you doing with Lisa Crocker?" I asked, instantly. Gamma and I had agreed that I would do most of the talking for fear that he might recognize her voice. She'd lived in Gossip much longer than me.

"L-Lisa?"

"Yes. Your cousin, Lisa. What were you doing with her?"

He swallowed nervously. I tightened my grip again.

Matthew let out a piggy squeal. "She was checking up on me. She didn't want me to say anything about..."

"About what?"

"About the job."

"Which job?" I growled.

Gamma shook her head at my theatrics.

"She hired me to break into her store and steal all her stuff," he replied. "Look, I don't want any trouble. I just did what she asked me to do. She paid me good for it and everything."

"Why did she ask you to rob her store?"

"I don't know."

"You didn't think to ask?" I raised an eyebrow at Gamma.

She shrugged.

"No. She told me it was none of my business. She gave me five hundred dollars and made me promise not to tell the cops, but I wasn't going to. Look, you're not the cops are you?"

"Don't worry about who we are," I said. "Worry that we'll find you again if you tell anyone about this." Fear worked better than money most of the time, sadly enough, not that Matthew was under any threat.

Gamma handed me an item and I frowned. It was a cookie in a brown paper bag.

"For the shock," she mouthed.

And Gamma thought I was a softie, sheesh. "What else can you tell us about Lisa?" I asked.

"Nothing. I don't know anything else. She just told me what to do, gave me the keys, and I did it."

No wonder there had been no signs of an external break-in. He had had the keys. And he had likely erased the footage, or perhaps Lisa had done that herself.

"Did you kill Barney Crocker?" I asked, on a whim.

Gamma rolled her eyes this time.

"No! I didn't hurt nobody."

"Yes, but did you hurt *somebody*?" Gamma asked, a stickler for grammar.

"No, ma'am. Say, don't I know you from somewhere?" Matthew turned his head, blindly, the silk sleeping mask comical given the situation.

"No, you don't," I answered for Gamma. "And if you talk about this…" I let the threat linger in the air and tightened my grip one last time. Finally, I shoved the cookie into his hands. "Eat this."

"What is it?"

"It's a cookie. Eat it. Sorry for the trouble and thanks for the information." I kicked the car door open and pushed him out, ripping the eye mask free. I shut the door before he could think to turn and look at us.

Gamma drove off and we turned the corner, a shocked Matthew, munching on a cookie, in our rearview mirror.

"He had big feet," I said.

"What on earth does that matter?"

"Shoe size," I replied, "is important in a murder investigation." The shoe prints in the soil beside the bush had been small for a man's feet, but still a man's. That ruled out Matthew. But that wasn't our problem.

Lisa had hired me to solve a case that didn't need solving. Why?

# Eleven

Confronting Lisa about her lies wouldn't get us anywhere, not without actual evidence that proved she'd been lying. Even then, there was a chance she'd deny everything. That had happened to me in a previous case, so I was well acquainted with the possibility.

But even if Lisa didn't cave and admit that she'd hired her cousin to break-in to her store, we needed the evidence to prove she had. Then we could take that evidence to the cops. Or drop off on Detective Goode's doorstep, mysteriously.

*Ugh, don't think about him.*

Every time I did, my heart would skip about twenty beats, and I'd lose track of my thoughts. A date. On Saturday. Was I really going to do that? Meet up with him and...

"Charlotte," my grandmother sang. "Where on earth are you?"

I shook my head, checking my seatbelt was correctly fastened as we sailed through the streets, heading back toward the inn.

"I'm right here," I said. "I was just thinking about the next steps. It's probably a good idea to go over to the Crocker household and find out what's going on. Maybe talk to Grandma Crocker."

"Dora's been staying with Barney for as long as I've lived in Gossip," Gamma said. "Though, she's more than able to pay for her own place and hire help if she needs it."

"That just makes me suspicious?"

"Why?" Gamma asked, her gaze fixed on the road ahead.

"Because she didn't seem that upset about the passing of her son. I imagine losing a child is devastating, no matter how old they are. If I think about losing one of the cats... anyway," I said, clearing my throat. "It just strikes me as strange."

"She did hire you to find out who did it," Gamma said.

"True."

"Dora's always been a tough cookie. I admire that in a woman."

I dropped the topic. Gamma, for all her professionalism, was defensive about friends and family, and I liked that about her. Besides, I didn't want to upset her so close to her birthday and Thanksgiving. Gosh, I had been so distracted by the cases I'd forgotten about all the Thanksgiving prep we needed to do after Project Unknown Number was complete.

We arrived back at the Gossip Inn, and Gamma parked the SUV in the spot that connected to her underground parking bay. She checked the coast was clear before we descended into darkness at the click of a button.

"You become more like Batman everyday," I said. "You know that?"

"Don't be absurd, Charlotte. You're no Alfred Pennyworth."

I certainly wasn't. Which brought me back to my concerns about my place in Gossip. Ugh. What was wrong with my brain?

Was it normal to get this much of a mental work out over worries?

Gamma and I changed out of our black gear in silence once we had reached the armory, and then proceeded upstairs. I picked a batch of mushrooms from the Shroom Shed for Lauren before heading to the kitchen.

"There you are, Charlie," Lauren said, looking up from the table. She wore the onion-cutting goggles and brandished a knife. "I was hoping you'd get back here in time for lunch."

I groaned at the prospect of more onion cutting, but took over from her, taking the opportunity to sit in silence and think about Lisa Crocker's strange behavior.

Lisa had declared that the cops wouldn't help her find the burglars. I would have to ask Goode about that. Did he know she'd been robbed? Surely. The news had traveled all over town within the hour.

Lisa had hired her cousin to do the robbing. Why? Insurance purposes, perhaps? Maybe she wanted to make a claim and get money to refurbish the store? But if that was the case, why trash it in the first place?

And what was with the cheap quality dress that had supposedly come from the Butterscotch Boutique.

Insurance fraud would make the most sense to me, but at the same time, why the cheap dresses? Why bother having the store robbed, if she wanted money? Why not burn the whole place down?

And what about Barney's death?

The lunch service passed in a blur, from the meal prep, to Lauren's chatting about the townsfolk, guests, and her plans for Gamma's cake, to serving the guests themselves. Gamma's surprise birthday party was in a few days, and we had arranged everything in record time, mostly thanks to Lauren.

After the kitchen was clean, I stripped off my apron and headed out the front door, my mind set on my next goal. To talk directly with Grandma Crocker without Lisa around.

The Crocker household was quiet, and there were no cars parked out front. A good sign for me. If Lisa had taken the Audi and it wasn't here... well, that had to mean she was still at the Butterscotch Boutique.

I hit the buzzer for the intercom and waited, impatiently.

"Hello? Who's there?" Grandma Crocker's voice crackled through the speaker.

"It's Charlotte Smith," I said. "I wanted to ask you a couple of questions about Lisa." There had been no love lost between the women the other day, and I was banking on that.

"Of course," Grandma Crocker replied. "Whatever I can do to help."

The gates clicked and swung inward and I started up the pathway. Grandma Crocker met me on her front porch, the calico cat in her arms. It purred and butted its head against her palms, occasionally mewing for more attention when she stopped petting it.

"How are you today, dear?" Grandma Crocker asked.

"I'm well thanks and you?"

"Terrible, given the circumstances. What do you want to know about Lisa? I assume it's related to my son's passing?"

"I guess you could say that." I told Grandma Crocker, briefly, about what I'd discovered. Lisa had lied about the break-in at her store, and her behavior had been suspicious. "So, my question to you is, did Barney have a life insurance policy?"

"No," Grandma Crocker said. "No, he didn't. My poor Barney was in financial trouble. After he retired, everything went downhill. No money to keep things afloat, you see, and I wanted to help but... he made it difficult."

"How so?"

"I told Barney that I would only help him if he forced Lisa to close that ridiculous Butterscotch Boutique. It was a time and money suck and wasn't making a profit. I assume that's still the case."

"And he refused?" I asked.

"Yes. My son wanted to give Lisa everything her heart desired. For whatever odd reason, he thought she was the best thing since sliced garlic bread." Grandma Crocker sighed. "And now she's had her store robbed? It sounds like insurance fraud to me. If that's the case, I doubt there's much she wouldn't do to get her hands on some cash."

"There have been reports that the boutique has been selling sub-par clothing under the guise of being designer wear. Do you know anything about that?"

"No. And I'm not sure how that's related to my son's death either," Grandma Crocker said.

Neither was I.

But there had to be a connection, and I firmly believed it was money. A motive that made sense. Unless the rumors of Lisa's affair were true.

"Do you know if Lisa was having an affair?" I asked.

"She might've been." Grandma Crocker put down the calico cat and straightened. "I never know with that woman. I've made it clear to her what I think of her, and I told Barney the same. The woman is... selfish beyond imagining."

"Did Lisa have a gun?"

"Not that I know of," Grandma Crocker replied. "But she didn't shoot Barney. I was right there with her. It was that redhead in the bushes."

"Best to check, regardless."

"Of course." Grandma Crocker wriggled her nose. "You know, maybe you can find something in Lisa's office. She usually keeps it locked, but..."

"But?"

"I assume that you'll be able to get into it, if you're a 'fixer' as everyone says."

So, Grandma Crocker was giving me outright permission to snoop in her daughter-in-law's office. Interesting.

"Sure," I said. "I can get in. Is the office on the first or second floor?"

"Second."

"And it's locked?" I asked.

"Sure is."

I backed off the porch. "Mind showing me which window belongs to Lisa's office?"

Grandma Crocker came down the steps, and I offered her a hand to help her. We proceeded into the yard and down the side of the house. The walls were covered in more of those creeper plants, bare thanks to fall. There was a trellis, a pipe that looked like it might take my weight, and the roof of the porch with plenty of roof tiles to slip on.

"There. That's it," Grandma Crocker said, pointing toward a second floor window that was open a crack.

"We're in luck."

"How so?"

I walked to the trellis, scaled it easily, jumped and caught hold of the ledge of the roof porch, then used my upper body strength to haul myself up onto it. I tightened my core muscles to help with my balance, hoping that all those extra lemon chiffon cupcakes wouldn't affect me too negatively.

Thankfully, I'd chosen to wear my sneakers today. I picked my way across the ceramic tiles and reached the second floor window that led into Lisa's office. Compared to getting down from the inn's attic, this was nothing.

"Goodness," Grandma Crocker said. "Goodness me."

"Be right back." I waved to her then entered the room beyond.

# Twelve

The interior of the office was neat as a pin.

Lisa kept everything in its place. That or she didn't use this place that much. If that was the case, why keep the door locked? There was no key in the door, no way for me to get out but to go back the way I'd come.

But first, I had to find the truth.

I scanned the room.

There was a bookcase with various non-fiction business books and memoirs, a desk with two drawers, a leather-backed chair, a view of the garden, and that was about it. No computer, so no interesting emails to peruse while I was up here.

Was Lisa the only one who'd used this office?

I started with the drawers because there was nowhere

else to start. No filing cabinets either. What was that about?

I pulled out my phone and shot off a text to Gamma, informing her of my discussion with Grandma Crocker in brief, then opened the top drawer in the desk.

It was packed full of papers. I pulled them out, my eyebrows climbing.

OK, so Lisa was *nowhere* as neat as I'd thought. The documents were receipts, disorganized in a pile, and several of them were from one place in particular.

Purchase slips from "Couture Clothing Wholesale."

I selected one of those receipts, dated from last week, and tucked it into the back pocket of my jeans. Then, I searched for the store online.

"What do we have here," I murmured.

*Couture Clothing Wholesale. Your one-stop shop for the best couture pieces at reduced prices. If you're looking for that one of a kind dress, but can't afford to shop at places that charge way too much for clothes, in the Couture Clothing Wholesale is for you!*

The cutesy description told me everything I needed to know.

Lisa had been getting her clothing, the supposed designer clothing that was meant to be exclusive, hand-made even, from a wholesale clothing store at a reduced price, then selling those clothes at a mark-up.

That was scammy as heck. But it didn't prove anything about Barney's murder.

The door to the office opened, and I turned, expecting that Grandma Crocker had found the key and decided to check on me.

Lisa crossed the threshold and stopped dead in her tracks, her hand on the doorknob. Her jaw dropped, eyes widening, her yellow hair frazzled. "What the—?"

"Hi." I put up a bright smile.

What was the point in denying I was up here, rummaging through her things? The papers were all over the desk, and there was no hiding my intentions.

"You... you..."

"Yes," I said. "I broke into your office to find out what you've been up to, Lisa."

"I'll call the cops."

"No, I don't think you will."

"Excuse me?"

"I don't think you will," I repeated. "You see, you're hiding too much from the police to call them. And I know exactly what you're hiding, Lisa."

Her chin wobbled, unattractively.

"Do you want to know what I know, Lisa?"

She didn't answer, but her knuckles were white on the door handle.

"I know that you've been buying cheap, knock-off

clothing and selling it to people in town. I know that you hired your cousin, Matthew Fellers, to rob your store, and I know, thanks to your own words on the day you hired me, that you're claiming damages from insurance," I said. "That's a lot of spectacularly illegal things in one fell swoop."

Mouth movements in response. No sound.

"So, Lisa, you see, we're in a bit of a predicament," I said. "You hired me to find out who robbed your store, and I've done so. I believe you owe me the other half of my fee now that the job is complete."

"How dare you! You broke into my house."

"Did I, though? Tell you what, Lisa, I'll be willing to waive my fee if you'll answer a few of my questions about your husband, and the man you're having an affair with." It was a wild guess, but I wanted a new lead. I still didn't have a connection between Lisa and the murder. I didn't have a real motive.

"Affair! I'm not having any affair! Barney was the only man for me."

"I don't know whether to believe you," I said, tilting my head to one side. "And I'm afraid I'm going to have to go to the police with the evidence I've found proving that you've been scamming people in town and committing insurance fraud." The last part, I didn't technically have evidence for, but I doubted she would call my bluff.

"I— I—"

"You, what?" I asked. "Why don't we cut to the chase here. Who did you hire to kill your husband?"

"What?!"

"Who did you hire to kill your husband? What was her name?"

"I didn't hire anyone," she said, gasping and clutching the string of pearls at her neck. "I would never have hurt Barney."

"Then why all the lies about the store?"

"Because I... I just wanted to keep the Butterscotch Boutique afloat. I couldn't afford it any other way," she said. "And I don't owe you an explanation about this. You're the one who broke into my house. So if you go to the police, so will I."

*Ugh. That's not good.* And she hadn't given me a clear enough answer either. "I don't get it, Lisa. How will ruining your product and damaging your store help you stay afloat. I doubt the insurance will pay that much."

She pressed her lips into a thin line. "I'm calling the cops," she said. "If you don't leave my house, right now, I'm calling the cops."

"Fine," I said. "I'll leave. But your conscience will catch up with you eventually. I know there's something you're not telling me. I'll find out what it is." I was seldom this threatening with suspects, but I'd been caught on the back foot. The best defense was a good offense, after all.

I brushed past Lisa and made my way down the stairs and out of the house into the front yard. Grandma Crocker was still around the side of the house, holding a hand to her forehead to shade her eyes from the sun, peering up at the window. She hadn't noticed Lisa arriving home.

I fetched her and brought her back to the porch before heading off, my mind a tangle.

Lisa had wanted money and had committed insurance fraud to get it, but I didn't buy that it was to keep the Butterscotch Boutique afloat. There had to be a deeper reason.

It was clear she had run out of money *long ago*, if the receipts upstairs from the wholesale store were anything to go by. She couldn't afford to stock designer clothing at all.

So why only commit insurance fraud now? Why when, by all rights, people still bought from the boutique, like Jemimah had?

I had to figure this out soon.

# Thirteen

*Two days later...*

"I'm sure there's more to it," I said to Gamma, as we stood in the incubator room. Jemimah was due to arrive at any moment, and Gamma had been checking on the smallest kittens, ensuring they didn't need any help.

With so few guests both in the inn and the cat hotel, we had more free time to contemplate. And it just happened to be my mission this morning to keep Gamma distracted until I could shuttle her through to the dining area where the surprise party had been set up.

"I agree," Gamma said, folding her arms. "So, Lisa

buys cheap clothing and sells it in the boutique. She does so for how long?"

"Months," I said, pulling the receipt from my back pocket. I had been carrying it with me every day. "This is the most recent purchase, but she's been doing this for literally months."

"I'd bet anything that her purchasing the cheap clothing coincided with Barney's retirement and return to Gossip," Gamma said. "She was trying to make a few extra dollars to fund the boutique."

"Grandma Crocker said the boutique was a time and money suck," I replied. "And that she doubted it was turning a profit. But, surely, such a huge mark-up would turn a profit for Lisa?"

"Yes, that should've helped her, though she might've suffered from less people coming into the store and more returns."

"Right," I said. "But still. There should've been a small boost of money. So why the insurance fraud? Why risk *everything* for such little reward."

"Now, Charlotte, you don't know how much Lisa was paid by her insurance company," Gamma replied, sagely. "For all we know, those clothes could've been insured for a lot."

I wriggled my nose from side-to-side. "True."

But I still had a gut feeling that something about this case was off. The back door of the kitten foster center, the one that wasn't connected to the inn proper, opened and shut. Jemimah appeared, smiling brightly, and stepped easily over the half-door that separated the older kittens from the incubation room. "Good morning," she sang. "How are you today?"

"Good, thanks," I said, then disappeared into my thoughts again.

Two days had passed since I'd confronted Lisa, and I'd found out nothing else. I had no clue who might've committed the murder. No leads on the redheads yet, though I was sure that Lauren would come back to me with a list soon. And even if she did, that still didn't explain the man wearing the hoodie that had left the shoe print at the scene.

I brought myself back to the present.

There were more important things to focus on right now. Like my grandmother's party.

"Come on, Georgina. Let's get some coffee. I need to pick your brain."

"Very well," Gamma said.

She followed me out into the hall, and I made for the dining room. Gamma followed, even though we usually took our coffee in the kitchen.

We entered the dining room and it erupted into noise and activity.

"Surprise!" The shout came from the guests gathered, from Lauren, Jason, and Josie, the local baker, to Quinton McLarkal, Grandma Crocker, and an array of other women and men I didn't recognize but who all knew and loved Gamma.

"Goodness me!" Gamma pressed a hand to her chest. "You took me entirely by surprise."

I narrowed my eyes at her. She winked at me.

"You didn't really think you could keep secrets from me, did you, Charlotte?" Gamma whispered, as she moved by.

"Don't tell Lauren," I replied.

The chef would be heartbroken if she discovered that Gamma had known about our birthday ruse all along. The dining area was decorated beautifully, with streamers and balloons, and a tiered tower of lemon chiffon cupcakes. Lauren had baked a cake as well, and decorated it with a fondant icing replica of the Gossip Inn.

There were gifts galore on a table off to one side, and we had cleared out the center of the dining area for dancing and chatter.

"I need your help in the kitchen, Charlie," Lauren said.

And I was swept off to help prepare the last of the finger foods. I helped Lauren lay out drinks and platters, to ensure that all the guests were fed and watered, and then I fetched Cocoa Puff, Sunlight, and Snowy, who had been upstairs in my room, waiting with their matching bow-ties clipped onto their collars.

"Oh, they look adorable, Charlotte." Gamma clapped her hands and kissed each of the kitties. "This is wonderful."

Jemimah stopped by to join the party, and the music started up. Fleetwood Mac. One of Gamma's favorite bands from her "wild child" days as she liked to call them.

I stood in the corner of the room, watching as my grandmother was drawn from one group of adoring friends to the next, all while snacking on treats and laughing happily.

She fit in.

My grandmother, the ex-spy, the woman who had brought down the heads of drug cartels, who was technically still in hiding during her retirement, fit in with these people. She belonged in this small town. She had made her home here. She had found a life that made her happy, even though it wasn't as action-packed as the past.

Could I really do the same? And could I do it while I was still living under her roof?

I swallowed nervously.

*There are other things to worry about.*

Like dates with detectives, and murder cases, and

insurance fraud. Too much to count. Would I ever be comfortable when—

The music cut off, and the guests protested. Everyone turned to find the source of the disturbance.

Detective Goode stood next to the stereo, his finger on the power button. "Sorry for interrupting your party, Georgina."

"What seems to be the problem, Detective?" Gamma asked, frowning.

Detective Goode approached me, his frown deep, his hand on the cuffs at his belt.

"Charlotte Smith, you're under arrest for Interfering with Public Duties. Turn around, hands behind your back."

My stomach dropped. Everyone in the room stared. Gamma opened her mouth, but I shook my head, turned, and put my hands behind my back.

# Fourteen

"YOU HAVE the right to remain silent." Detective Goode sat in the interrogation room at the Gossip Police Station, holding the card with my Miranda Rights on it. "Anything you say can and will be used against you in a court of law. You have the right to an attorney. If you cannot afford an attorney, one will be appointed to you by the court. You can decide at any time to exercise these rights and not answer any questions or make any statements. Do you understand each of these rights I have explained to you?"

"Yes," I said.

"Bearing these rights in mind, would you like to talk to us now?" Goode's back was facing the door, his green-eyed gaze boring into me. Another officer sat on the other side of the room, arms folded atop his protruding belly, watching me.

I licked my lips. "Yes," I said. "I'll talk to you."

"All right." Detective Goode didn't look that happy about having to talk to me. "So, let me explain what's going on here, just so we're on the same page."

"OK." I already knew what was going on. He'd caught me interfering in his case, and unlike Detective Crowley, who'd never had the plums to arrest me, he was doing it. Even though he'd asked me on a date.

Needless to say, that was friggin' cancelled.

"We were approached by a distressed witness in a murder case," Goode said, "who claimed that you have been hired by another witness to investigate the death of Mr. Barney Crocker. Do you understand?"

I stared at him without answering.

"I need to know that you heard what I said."

"I heard what you said," I replied.

"Good. Investigating the case and removing items from the Crocker household constitutes disturbing the duties of a peace officer," Detective Goode said, and opened the dossier on his desk. He removed a plastic sleeve containing the receipt I had taken from Lisa's home. "Given that this was removed from the Crocker household by you, of course."

I didn't comment. He wanted me to admit that I'd removed the item, and thus had disrupted his case.

I could make several deductions thanks to this arrest.

First, that the receipt I had removed from the house was related to the murder case. Second, that they were in close contact with Lisa. Third, that they had released the house but were surveilling it because they had suspicions about Lisa Crocker or Grandma Crocker. Fourth, this had to be important if they were interviewing me.

Interfering with Public Duties was a Class B Misdemeanor. I knew because I'd done my research since I happened to interfere with public duties with increasing regularity. And they couldn't arrest me without real evidence. That was what warrants were for.

So, they might as well march me in front of a judge, set my bail, tell me my court date and be done with it.

Yet, I was here. Being interviewed by detectives in a gray interrogation room with a plastic table, drinking water out of a Styrofoam cup.

"What do you want to talk to me about?" I asked.

"You removed this from Lisa Crocker's home," Detective Goode said. "Why?"

"If I help you," I replied, "will the charges against me be dropped?"

"I can't say whether that will happen."

I shut my mouth.

"You understand the seriousness of interfering with public duties, right? It might be a misdemeanor, but it carries a potential punishment of a fine of $2,000 or up to six months in prison. And withholding information from a police officer can be tacked onto that."

"I'd like to talk to an attorney now," I replied, stiffly.

Detective Goode wilted, and, for a second, I got the impression he was relieved. Maybe he didn't want to spend more time in this room with me than he had to.

BY THE TIME I was released, it was 10:00 p.m., and my eyes were heavy with exhaustion. Gamma picked me up in her Mini, her expression grim, and we spent the first portion of our drive in silence.

"It won't stick, Charlotte, if that's what you're concerned about," Gamma said, at last.

I turned my head, studying my stoic grandmother's side-profile. Even now, she was regal. Even after my arrest had ruined her birthday party. That was what stung the most. Lauren and I had spent so much time planning it. We'd been so excited.

"The charges," Gamma continued. "They won't stick. Don't you worry, I have friends in high places who will ensure that."

"I'm not worried," I said. "Detective Goode was correct to arrest me. I did interfere."

"Because you were hired to do so."

"I understand that I tread a moral line and step over it too," I replied, sighing, "and I'll take my punishment for it. I mean, it was bound to happen some time, right?"

Gamma shook her head. "I won't stand for it. What happened at the station. Did you talk to them?"

I told her about my experience, and Gamma nodded. "Ah. So they want you to help them by giving them testimony about what you did. They're onto Lisa then."

"That's what I thought," I replied. "They believe that she was the one who committed the murder."

"Then, we've got to prove it," Gamma said, roughly. "We'll prove it without a shadow of a doubt. That way, Detective Goode will have no choice but to drop the charges against you. My research tells me that you being willing to help them solve a case will count in your favor. Might lead to the prosecutor dropping the charges against you entirely. But... either way, I won't let this stand."

"I don't want you to endanger yourself, Georgina."

"Don't be silly, Charlotte. Family is family." Gamma parked the Mini-Cooper outside the inn then got out, her nose in the air. I'd never seen her this way before. Guarded, angry, defensive, even, and all because of me.

"I've done as much as I can to prove it was her," I said. "We've tailed her, kidnapped her cousin, broken into her home, interviewed her, interviewed her mother-in-law, and even stolen proof that she was doing illegal stuff with the boutique. I don't see what other options there are."

"We'll figure it out," Gamma said. "Trust me."

I did. That was what made this so difficult. I felt terrible about Gamma having to give up her time on her special day because of me. "I'm sorry your birthday was ruined."

"Nonsense," Gamma said. "It was lovely. I got the gift you and Lauren organized, and it was perfection! Now, let's go inside and figure out how we're going to prove that Lisa Crocker killed her husband." She looped her arm through mine and guided me up the inn's front steps.

With Gamma on my side, I couldn't possibly be hopeless. That was like being unhappy about a locked door when you had a skeleton key.

# Fifteen

"I don't like this," I said, sitting in the back of the black SUV. "It feels wrong."

"I'll be fine, Charlie." Lauren was in the passenger seat, wearing a cute frock and clutching the ruined silk dress that Jemimah had given me. "I can do it. I promise."

"It's not about you not being able to do it," I said. "It's about you endangering yourself. Lisa could be the killer."

"I've always wanted to do this cool spy stuff you two are talking about." Lauren turned in her seat, meeting me stare for stare. "And now I get to."

My grandmother didn't comment as she drove us down the road, heading into town. We had woken early, served the guests breakfast, then headed down into the armory. Lauren's eyes had nearly bugged out of her head at the sight of the high-tech gear, but she'd taken it pretty well.

This was the first time Gamma had allowed her to see it. Or to participate in a mission.

But desperate times...

Gamma and I would be recognized too easily, and Lisa would become suspicious if we went anywhere near the boutique.

"So," Lauren said, "what's my cool codename? Wait, what are *your* cool code names?"

"I'm Chaplin. Georgina is Big G."

"Then I want to be, uh, Scarlett! Can I be Scarlett? Like Scarlett O' Hara. I do declare." She fanned her face then grinned at us.

"Sure," I said.

Gamma parked down the road from the Butterscotch Boutique, then turned toward Lauren. "I've already debriefed you, but I'm going to go over this one last time," she said. "To make sure that this goes off without a hitch."

"Got it, Big G." Lauren giggled and plastered her hand over her mouth.

*Oh boy, this is not going to go well.*

"You're already wearing your microphone, as are we," Gamma said. "We'll be directing you step-by-step, and we'll be able to see everything you do using the micro-camera attached to the front of your dress.'

"Yeah. Got it."

"You are to enter the boutique, find Lisa, and complain about the dress your friend bought. Lead her away from her purse or her phone. Once she's out of sight, I'll take over and place the bug on her phone."

"You can do that from a distance?" Lauren asked.

"Yes," Gamma said. "All you have to do is distract her. Got it, Scarlett?"

"Roger that!" Lauren did a comical salute then let out a breath. "Oh boy, I'm super nervous. How do y'all do this on a daily basis?"

"You get used to it eventually," I said.

That or you saw some extremely upsetting things and got over your fears once you realized just how terrible the world could be. That was the appeal of Gossip, wasn't it?

"OK," Lauren said. "I think I'm ready, Big G." No giggling this time.

"Then go for it."

Lauren checked the coast was clear before emerging onto the sidewalk and walking off. Nobody appeared to care where she'd come from or pay her any mind. She crossed the street, and disappeared into the Butterscotch Boutique.

Gamma tapped the screen on the SUV's dashboard and brought it to life. Within seconds, we had Lauren's camera feed and audio from her microphone on screen. I climbed into the front seat to get a better view.

"Good morning," she said, as Lisa joggled into view. "How are you today?"

"Oh, hello," Lisa replied. "Are you new to the Butterscotch Boutique? I haven't seen you here before." The words were sniffy, as if Lisa had weighed Lauren up and decided she probably couldn't afford to shop at the boutique.

"I'm new, sure, I guess you could say that." Lauren walked past Lisa and toward the back of the store, but not before she angled her body so that we caught sight of Lisa's purse sitting on the glass counter near the front of the boutique.

"Clever," I whispered.

"She's a smart girl," Gamma replied. "I always had faith she'd perform well under pressure. One can't have two children and run a kitchen without nerves of steel."

Lauren stopped near a clothing rack far from the purse and the front counter then cleared her throat. "My friend shops here, actually. Jemimah?"

"Oh, I remember her, yeah. Bought a beautiful silk dress from us," Lisa simpered.

"Right. Except that's what I kind of need to talk to you about," Lauren said. "Sorry, but... could you come take a look at this."

Lisa approached, leaving the front of the store empty, the door ajar to allow new customers easy access.

Gamma cut the feed from Lauren's video, though we could still hear the audio through our earpieces. My grandmother removed the FlyBoy Drone™ from the center console of the SUV, along with its tiny remote. She opened the window and tossed the drone into the air.

The video feed on the screen appeared—video footage of the street from above— and my grandmother directed the drone, with its fisheye lens, into the store through the open door. She flew the drone toward the purse and into it.

"Can't see a thing," I said.

"No problem." Gamma clicked a button on her remote, and a green haze descended over the screen.

"Night vision? Since when?"

"New hardware update," Gamma winked. "And Rodrigo added a little something extra for me too, that'll come in handy with our mission."

"What is it?"

"Remote connection to devices via Bluetooth," she replied.

The drone descended into the purse and we got a close-up view of a lipstick tube, scrunched up receipts and, finally, Lisa's phone. Gamma sat the drone directly on top of it and hit another button on the remote. She reached over and did the same with the screen.

Lisa's phone's interface appeared on the screen.

"You're kidding," I said. "You hacked her phone? With the drone?"

"Poetry," Gamma replied. "But not quite hacking. Remote control. Now, all I have to do is install a special piece of software." She tapped buttons on the screen then inserted what appeared to be a micro-drive into the side of it. A bar appeared on the screen, flashing, with the words uploading underneath it.

In the interim, Lauren had been complaining at length about the dress. I tuned back into the conversation, listening in case Lisa decided to head back toward the purse.

Likely, she wouldn't be too bothered about a fly in her purse, but if she saw the light of her phone from within her purse, she might check who was "calling" her.

"—love to help you, but there's no evidence that this item of clothing is even from the boutique," Lisa said. "I don't remember selling that to Jemimah. I sold her silk, and this is a strange hybrid material that I simply don't stock in my store."

"She's such a liar," I muttered.

"Well, I think you should give my friend a refund. She has the receipt for the purchase, you know."

"Then where is it?" Lisa asked.

"Jemimah has it."

"I'm afraid I can't help you."

I glanced at the upload bar. It was nearly done, but not quite there yet.

"Distract her, Scarlett," I breathed. "We're not done yet."

"Wait," Lauren said, hastily. "Wait a second."

"Let go of me, this instant," Lisa snapped.

"I will when you give me a refund. This isn't OK. You're taking advantage of the people in this town, selling them poor quality items."

"How dare you!"

The upload completed, Gamma locked the screen, and then flew the drone out of the purse.

"We're done, Scarlett," I said.

"Sorry," Lauren said, immediately. "I'll go back to Jemimah and get the receipt." The sound of her breathing dominated the microphone as she exited the boutique, clutching the faux-silk dress in hand.

Gamma flew the drone out in front of her and back to the car. She put her palm out the window and landed the bug in it. "All right," she said, placing the FlyBoy back into the center console with a couple of taps. "Mission success. Now, all we have to do is listen in on her calls."

I shifted into the back to give Lauren her seat back.

Lauren got back into the SUV, pink-cheeked. "What a horrible woman," she said. "Horrible."

"You did great," I said. "Really great."

The resulting beam of joy lifted my spirits. It was good to see her happy, and the mission had been a success, even if I'd felt like I'd done nothing to help.

<h1 style="text-align:center">Sixteen</h1>

"You know what I want, Crocker." The man's voice was thick, New York accent, maybe Brooklyn?

"I need more time," Lisa replied, crystal clear through the phone.

Lauren, Gamma, and I sat around the worn kitchen table in the Gossip Inn, Cocoa Puff, Snowy, and Sunlight watching from the entrance to the room. Gamma's phone was on the table between us, the call between Lisa and whoever this guy was clear as day.

"I don't like having to chase after people, understand? I don't like having to do extra work to get what I'm owed," he said.

"This is so cool," Lauren whispered. "I can't believe you managed to bug her phone while I was talking to her. How did you even do that?"

Gamma lifted a finger to her lips.

"Mr. Cole, I'm doing everything I can right now. It's been a tough week. There was a break-in at my store, you see."

"I don't want to hear no excuses," Mr. Cole spat. "I loaned you the money you needed, you said you'd pay me back, and you didn't. That's like... spitting in the face of a dying man. Don't make me send my associate over to talk to you again."

"Please. I just need... another week."

"You've got twenty-four hours. You don't get me my money, there'll be consequences." And then the line went dead.

Gamma reached over and stopped the recording. Ever since we'd bugged Lisa's phone, she'd been recording every single call that had come through, no matter how benign it seemed.

"A loan shark," I said. "She owes money to a loan shark."

"That would explain why she was committing insurance fraud. She's afraid of what the loan shark will do to her."

"Or to Barney."

Gamma and I stared at each other. Lauren gulped, audibly. Had the loan shark murdered Barney in cold blood? If so, surely he would've told Lisa about it. Surely,

Lisa would be more afraid than she'd sounded on the call.

Sure, her voice had been shaky, but it hadn't been "you murdered my husband" shaky.

"What do we do now?" Lauren asked.

"You don't do anything, Laur," I replied. "You've got a family to take care of. You've done your part."

"You can't exclude me now. I want in on this."

Gamma gave the chef a stern look. "You are not to put yourself in any danger. Charlotte and I can't focus when we're uncertain about your whereabouts or safety. Regardless, I need you to organize everything for Thanksgiving dinner. Quinton will be attending, as will a *special* guest. So I'll expect a meal for us, two guests, and your husband and children, of course." Gamma was putting her to work to keep her distracted.

Lauren pouted and pushed up from the table. "Fine. I guess I'd better get to planning then." She took her sacred recipe book out of the cupboard and set it on the countertop, placing her fists either side of it.

"We need to find out more about this guy," I said. "He's got to be new to town. But he seems oddly familiar. I don't know why, though."

"He's definitely new. I don't recognize him one bit. It's strange that you do." Gamma drew her phone closer. "I'm going to do some research on this man. Find out where he's located."

"That sounds like a great idea." The minute she had that information, I'd be paying Mr. Cole a visit. I wasn't about to let anyone do my dirty work, and while Gamma clearly wanted to keep me safe, I wasn't going to sit back.

Mr. Cole was about to meet his maker.

MR. COLE's office was in the center of town, in a two-story office building, on the first floor. He didn't have a nameplate on the door, and his receptionist was a woman who cared more about her phone than about his appointments.

I walked right past her desk, no complaints or questions, and knocked on his door.

"Yeah? Who's that?"

I let myself inside and shut the door behind me.

Gamma had told me the brief, ugly truth about Mr. Cole. He was from Brooklyn, New York, he was in the business of giving out loans, and he had one prior conviction for agg assault.

"Who the heck are you?" he asked, focusing bright blue eyes on me.

Recognition slammed home, and I inhaled, sharply.

This guy! This was the guy I'd seen outside Lisa's boutique at the beginning of the week. The guy with the slicked back hair, the open-collared shirt showing off his chest and the gold chain he wore around his neck.

"Mr. Cole," I said. "Nice to meet you."

"I know you?" he asked, pointing a stubby finger at me. "Jimmy!" That was shouted toward the door.

It opened behind me and another man entered the room. A goofy guy wearing jeans two sizes too small, who was sweating profusely.

Another shock of recognition.

This second guy? I'd seen him in Lisa's boutique the other day too. She'd said his name was Mr. Dolgner, and he was shopping for a dress for his wife. Clearly, that had been a life. This had to be one of the loan shark's associates or enforcers.

*Killers? But where does the redhead come into it?*

The puzzle pieces didn't quite fit.

"Hey, Jimmy boy, take a seat, will ya?" Mr. Cole said. "We've got us a client, looks like."

"OK, boss." Jimmy's accent was Texan. He sat on a chair in the corner, folding his meaty, sweaty arms. The sour odor of him filled the room, quick.

"You'll have to excuse my associate," Mr. Cole said. "He's got some personal issues that prevent him from ever smelling like anything other than a truck full of horse manure."

Jimmy wasn't in the least bit fazed by the insult.

Mr. Cole got up and opened the tiny window behind his desk, then faced me again. "So, what can I do you for?" he asked. "You lookin' for money, sweet cheeks?"

"You're Mr. Cole," I said, smiling as sweetly as I could manage. "A friend of mine recommended I should talk to a Mr. Cole about a loan."

"Oh yeah? That's a good friend you got. Right, Jimmy?"

"With friends like that, who needs enemies, right, boss?" Jimmy guffawed.

"Shut up, idiot." Mr. Cole flashed me yellowing teeth. "Yeah, honey, I'm Mr. Cole. Buddy Cole. Baby Eyes to the ladies." He winked at me.

*Don't throw up in your mouth. Focus.* "I'm Charlotte Smith," I said.

"Nice to meet you, Charlie. Mind if I call you that?"

"Yes," I said. "I'd prefer it if you called me Charlotte."

"Well, now, that's no problem. Wanna take a seat?" He gestured, rather unctuously, toward a worn faux-leather chair in front of his desk.

"I'm fine standing, thanks."

"Suit yourself." He heaved himself into his own

creaking chair and sat back, plastering his hands behind his head. "Now, what seems to be the problem.

I glanced down at his feet beneath the desk, then at his associates. They both had relatively small feet for men. Could it be?

It seemed likely.

"As I understand it," I said, "you recently loaned a woman by the name of Lisa Crocker a sum of money. How much did you loan her, exactly."

The oily grin vanished. "Don't know what you're talking about, honey. I don't know a Lisa."

"Oh, but you do," I replied. "You know her very well. You've been threatening her for a while now."

Mr. Cole snorted. "Even if I was, what's a little girl like you going to do about it?"

*Patience. Don't throat punch him. It won't get you anywhere.* "Nothing," I replied. "I'm not going to do anything. You see, Lisa also owes me money. I wanted to find out how much she owed you, see if maybe we could work together to extra a payday from her. I'm willing to do whatever it takes."

"Whatever it takes?" Mr. Cole rocked forward and back, hands still behind his head.

"Sure," I replied. "I heard that her husband's been murdered. Good riddance, am I right?"

No answer.

"I take it that was your work?"

"Nope," Mr. Cole said.

But was he lying?

"I don't do that kind of thing," Mr. Cole replied, narrowing his eyes at me. He didn't trust me, obviously. "You don't want any money from me, I'm going to have to ask you to leave. That or get escorted out by my sweaty associate over there. Trust me, you don't want his hands on you. Soak right through your clothes."

"How much did she loan from you?" I asked, a final time.

"It was enough." And that was the only answer I'd get out of him.

But I had new suspects, now. Ones that were more than capable of murder. Mr. Cole watched me like a hawk as I left the office.

Seventeen

"Slimy piece of work," I said, sipping my pumpkin spiced latte on the bench under the oak tree.

Gamma sat beside me drinking from her own cup. Lauren had made them for us in her frenzy of Thanksgiving preparations. She's already started setting up a menu and giving us food items to try out.

"Man, these are good." I took a sip. "Lauren's outdone herself again."

"I think she's making them angrily," Gamma replied. "She's mad she can't be a part of the rest of our investigation."

"Ugh, I knew involving her was a bad idea. Don't get me wrong, she did an amazing job with Lisa at the boutique, but I feel bad now. That kind of adrenaline rush isn't easy to forget about," I said. "You and I both know that."

"That's why I drink lattes," Gamma said. "Coffee is a great rush replacement."

I kicked my feet along the ground, shifting leaves and grass with the undersides of my boots. Mr. Cole had given me the creeps. So had his sweaty friend. But I had no proof that they'd done anything to Barney Crocker.

"What if I'm wrong," I said. "What if Grandma Crocker lied about there being a redhead on the scene, all so that she could throw us off her scent."

"You think this was Dora?"

"I'm just saying. What if?"

"Highly unlikely," Gamma said. "What would her motive be? She has plenty of money. She would never kill her only son. She adored him, even if she's rough around the edges."

I sighed. "What if... what if she wasn't trying to kill her son?" I asked. "What if she hired someone to murder Lisa?"

Gamma took a long drink of latte in response to that.

"What if she wanted to get rid of Lisa to free her son?" I continued. "Because she knew that Barney would always give Lisa everything they wanted. That must be difficult to watch, as a mother. Your son, trapped by a woman wasting all his money while you stand by and watch it happen?"

"It's an interesting theory," Gamma said. "But it's just that, Charlotte. A theory. No proof."

"No proof of anything except money borrowed and insurance fraud. All roads point to Lisa or these loan sharks," I said. "But it's off. The pieces don't fit."

"Perhaps."

"What do you think?" I asked.

"Lauren is on the way over and she looks enraged." Gamma's gaze was fixed on the inn.

I followed her gaze and found Lauren, marching across the front yard toward us, a piece of paper flapping in one hand, her cheeks red and her eyes blazing.

"Uh oh. What's that about?"

"We're about to find out, I'm afraid," Gamma said.

"You two think you can just involve me and then shut me out?" Lauren asked, the minute she'd stopped in front of us. "Think again!" She thrust the page toward me.

"What's this?" I frowned, lifting it.

"That is my research," Lauren replied, folding her arms over her chef's whites. "I know y'all are out here discussing the case without me, and that's a mistake."

"Research?" Gamma peered over my shoulder at the page.

"At the beginning of this week, Charlie asked me to compile a list of all the redheads in Gossip. The women, of course, because of what Grandma Crocker said about there being a woman at the crime scene." Lauren gave a delicate shudder at the phrase 'crime scene.' "And I did even better than that."

The list of names was short, and most of them had been crossed out.

"I got every single redheads alibi for the night of the murder, except for two," Lauren said, and pointed to the only two names on the list that weren't crossed out. "Jill Hardbody and Kimberly Brown."

"Wow," I said. "Lauren, this is amazing. You did this by yourself?"

"I sure did. I even wrote down all their alibis. It wasn't that difficult. We had a meeting of the Redhead Union, so I just asked them all."

"And they all had a valid alibi except for those two women?" Gamma asked, pointing delicately to the names that weren't crossed out.

"Correct," Lauren said. "Except, I know that one of them can't possibly have done it."

"Why?"

"Because she's dead."

*Goodness.* "Dead?" I asked.

"She died two weeks ago of old age. Died her hair red right to the end, old Jill did. She was such a delight too. Always willing to try new recipes or experiment with flavors." Lauren's anger faded and she grew emotional, lifting the end of her apron and dabbing beneath her eyes. "Anyway, the point is, Jill couldn't have been at the crime scene, so that just leaves Kimberly."

I stared at the name on the sheet.

*Kimberly Brown.*

I didn't recognize the name. And I certainly wasn't sure if she was connected to Lisa.

"Do you know her, Georgina?" I asked.

"I know of her. She works at the local convenience store," she said.

"Wait, isn't that where Lisa's cousin works?" My pulse ticked up a notch, if that was the case, did we finally have a connection between Lisa and the death of her husband? Could it really be a murder for hire plot?

"Yes, he works at the Diddle Doddle," Gamma said. "But that doesn't mean there's a connection."

"But the fact that she's the only adult redhead in town who doesn't have a solid alibi must mean that she's a suspect. Lauren, this is fantastic." I got up, nearly splashing pumpkin spiced latte down the front of my sweater.

The chef colored a pleasant pink. "Well, I just thought you should know that I'm not hopeless. That I can be of help. You don't need to treat me like I'm just... I don't know."

"Sorry," I said.

I knew what it was like to feel as if you didn't really have a purpose. Or that you weren't good enough.

"I really appreciate this, Lauren. More than I can even express," I said. "I was feeling so trapped, and this is one string I can officially follow. Grandma Crocker swore she saw a redhead at the scene. And now, we'll find out if she was telling the truth."

Eighteen

THE DIDDLE DODDLE convenience store was another new addition to Gossip, and it was slowly gaining popularity. It was kind of nice that more people were moving to town. The economy might not have been great, but that meant a lot of the younger generation were moving back with their parents, finding jobs, and bringing a new feeling of vibrance to town.

I parked the Mini-Cooper outside the Diddle Doddle, with its pink and white striped awning over the door, the shopping carts lined up neatly outside, and got out.

*This is it.*

The redhead was inside the store, and I just had to find her. I wasn't in the mood to pretend to be shopping. I wanted to get this over and done with, even if it meant an argument.

I entered the Diddle Doddle and scanned the cashiers at the front. There were five in total, standing next to their stations, and one of them had fiery red hair.

Kimberly was short and squat, her teeth yellow and chipped, but her eyes bright. She smiled as I approached.

"Welcome to the Diddle Doddle, ma'am," she said, brushing off her pink-striped apron. "May I help you with something today?"

*Friendly.* I usually trusted my gut instincts, and Kimberly wasn't giving me a bad vibe. She seemed sweet, even.

"You're Kimberly?" I glanced at her name tag for confirmation.

"Yes, I am, ma'am. What can I help you with?"

"What were you doing at the Crocker household on the night of Barney Crocker's murder?" I didn't know whether I'd lost patience with myself, the town, Detective Goode, or if I was just tired of dancing around the topic with everyone, especially since nobody had given up their info this week. That was how the question came out.

Kimberly's warm and welcoming smile disappeared. She blinked, stared at me blankly for a second, then took off running.

"Hey!" I yelled. "Hey! Come back!" I chased after her.

For a woman in a cashier's smock, she ran like the wind. It didn't help that Lauren had been force-feeding me gravy, lemon chiffon cakes, pumpkin spiced lattes, and pumpkin pie today. I sprinted, pumping my arms back and forth.

Kimberly led me across the parking lot and down the street. She took corners at speed, nearly tilting, slipping and falling in her haste. She drew level with the dog park, where pets yapped and played, and vaulted over the fence. Her smock got caught on it and tore free.

I followed her with what I hoped was a little more grace.

"Wait," I shouted. "Hey, wait a second." I was gaining on her.

Kimberly cast terrified glances over her shoulder. A bad idea. Her foot snagged a rock and she pitched forward, her arms pinwheeling.

The change in momentum was too sudden for me to anticipate.

I slammed into Kimberly, my arms latching onto her waist, and we toppled to the ground.

"Get off me!" she yelped. "Get off."

"No shot," I replied, and rolled her over onto her front. I sat on top of her, pinning her arms to her side, while concerned dog owners and walkers watched us from all around the park.

I waved at them. "Nothing to see here. She's, uh, she's my cousin." Lamest excuse ever. "Kimberly Brown."

"What are you, a cop?"

"No," I replied. "I'm worse than a cop. I'm a fixer."

"What's that?" She grimaced the words out.

*The arrogance of the youth today.* "Look," I said, "I want the truth. Why were you there that night. Why were you at the Crocker household. Did you shoot him?"

"No!"

"Then why were you there?"

"I'm not talking. You can't make me talk. I want a lawyer."

"I told you," I said, "I'm not a cop. And you're not going to get a lawyer before you talk to me. I want answers, Kimberly, and I'll do whatever it takes to get them. A man is dead, and if you were the one who did it..."

"I swear, it wasn't me, OK?"

"But you were there that day," I said. "That evening."

"Yeah, I was there."

"Why?"

Kimberly plastered her lips together, going white. She shook her head from side-to-side.

"Why?" I insisted.

*I should've brought some of Gamma's truth serum with me.*

"Tell me," I growled.

"Because Jimmy was there," she wailed, at last. I didn't know if she was afraid because of the look on my face or if the guilt of holding it in had gotten to her. "Jimmy was there, OK? I followed him."

"Jimmy?"

"My boyfriend, Jimmy Dolgner."

*Ah. Ah-ha.* Jimmy Dolgner, the sweaty enforcer for Mr. Cole had been at the Crocker residence on the night of the murder.

"Why was he there?" I asked.

"I thought he was having an affair," she said. "He'd been going to see this woman a lot lately at the boutique. At first, I thought it was 'cos he was going to buy me something special for my birthday, but that came and passed and he got me a pen." She wriggled one arm free and grabbed at the top pocket of her shirt. She produced a pen. "See? It says 'I heart New York' on it. Can you believe that?"

"How did you know Jimmy had been visiting the boutique?"

Kimberly's cheeks went the same color as her hair. "I followed him. Look, don't judge me. My ex-boyfriend had two affairs while we were dating. I'll never let a man treat me like that again. Never."

"So you've been stalking your boyfriend."

"Sure," she said. "I put a tracker app on his phone that tells me where he is at all times. I noticed that he kept going to the boutique a lot and then he started going to that address. Her house. So, I decided I'd follow him and find out what he was doing."

"And what did you see?" I asked.

Kimberly paled. "I saw... I saw a man get shot."

"Who shot him?"

She turned her head away. "I don't know."

"You can't protect him, Kimberly. He did the wrong thing. You have to tell the truth. An innocent man lost his life because of your boyfriend, you realize that, right?"

Kimberly didn't answer me.

"The cops are going to want more details."

Still silence.

"Who shot Mr. Crocker?" I asked.

"It was Jimmy, OK?" she said, miserably, the pen falling from her fingertips. "It was Jimmy. And I've been too scared to say anything about it to anybody because what if he does the same thing to me."

"He won't," I replied, getting off her and offering her a hand. "I'll make sure of that."

# Nineteen

*That night...*

"Come in, Big G," I said, as I approached the front of the building. "Confirm status."

"Operation Baby Shark is a go," Gamma replied in my ear, softly. "Suspect is inbound and should be arriving in t-minus five minutes."

Operation Baby Shark, our code name for taking down Mr. Cole or "Baby Blues" as he'd lovingly referred to himself, was simple. Lure the loan shark and his associate back to his office, enter, detain, leave the evidence we had on the scene after a brief interrogation of the suspects.

Gamma had called Mr. Cole and told him that she

desperately needed to meet with him. She'd played the part of an elderly woman who had no idea what she was getting herself into. A woman who wanted to put her dear grandchild through college but couldn't afford it.

Of course, scumbag Cole had gone for it instantly and agreed to meet her at his office at 09:00 p.m., even though it was after hours.

I slipped a silver pill into the lock on the front door of the office building then squeezed. The mechanism within shot out and unlocked the door. I entered the darkness within, shut the door again behind me, and made for the office.

Another door, another lock easily opened.

"Suspect is approaching." Gamma wore black and watched from the corner in the SUV.

"I'm in the office," I breathed, shutting the door. I stood behind it, pulling the balaclava down over my face. It was hot, and the office still smelled sour from what I assumed with Jimmy Dolgner's unfortunate body odor problem.

Boy, Kimberly really could do so much better than a murdering, sweat-monster who worked for a loan shark. Not that there was anything wrong with sweating a lot, especially if it was a medical condition, but the other stuff? Yeah, nothing medical about that.

"They've parked outside the building and are on their way in. Prepare yourself, Chaplin."

"Wilco, Big G."

The door to the building opened and slammed, and footsteps approached. I relaxed my muscles into a state of readiness. Tensing would only make things worse.

The door to the office opened, and the lights clicked on.

Mr. Cole entered first, heading toward his desk, and Jimmy followed right after. I stepped up behind the sweaty man and struck him in the neck, using the technique Gamma had taught me. A nerve pinch that would render him unconscious without the need for choking. Jimmy collapsed to the floor, instantly.

Mr. Cole spun around, wide-eyed. He let out a yell. I removed a gun from the holster on my hip in a fluid, practiced motion. It felt as normal to me as lifting a cup of coffee to my lips. An action that I had taken so many times, I had lost count.

"In the chair, Mr. Cole, quickly."

"Who the heck are you?"

"Chair. Now," I said, and removed a silencer from the utility belt around my pants. The entire get-up was made out of bullet-resistant material. Another set of items from my Gamma's armory. I screwed the silencer onto the end of the gun, calmly, and the sight appeared to convince Mr. Cole to comply.

He sat down in the chair.

I walked around to his side of the desk and removed cable ties from my pocket. I fastened his hands and then his ankles together before returning to do the same to Jimmy on the floor. The man was drooling and snorted in his unconscious state.

I rolled him over, dragged him up against the wall, and propped him upright.

"Status, Chaplin?"

"We're good," I breathed.

Mr. Cole watched me through narrowed eyes.

"Who are you?" he asked. "You one of Jack's guys?"

I shut the office door and locked it, then removed a recording device from my pocket and hit the button on it.

"Mr. Cole," I said, "did you or did you not hire Jimmy Dolgner to shoot Barney Crocker?"

"What? No, I didn't."

I lifted the gun and fired a shot into the potted plant on his desk. The ceramic pot exploded, and Mr. Cole screamed blue murder.

"Mr. Cole," I repeated. "Did you or did you not hire Jimmy Dolgner to shoot Barney Crocker?" This time, I aimed the weapon at his head.

Cole swallowed, his beady gaze flickering from the gun in my hand to my eyes. "I hired him to scare the woman, Lisa. That's it. I didn't say nothing about shooting. I didn't say nothing about murder. If he killed him, that's on him."

I holstered my gun, momentarily, then removed a pill from my pocket and rounded the desk.

"Hey, what are you doing? Hey!"

I shoved the pill between his teeth, then forced them together, like forcing a dog to swallow its medicine. The gritty crunch told me the pill had popped.

"What the heck are you—" Cole's eyes rolled back in his head, and he passed out.

Unlike the smack to the neck I had executed with Jimmy, the pill would keep Cole unconscious for a specific amount of time. And it was less dangerous. The dose was undetectable in the blood, too.

Jimmy was still out cold, so I walked over to him, removed my gun from its holster again, and pressed the cold metal against his cheek.

"Dolgner," I said, loudly. "Dolgner." I tapped his cheek hard—no bruising or pain. I didn't need Detective Goode mad because I'd hurt his suspect. "Dolgner, wake up."

The murderer's eyes opened. "Wh-what?"

"Jimmy Dolgner," I said, "I've been informed that you

shot Mr. Barney Crocker by your boss, Mr. Cole. Is that true?"

"W-what?"

I backed up a few steps and aimed the gun at him. "Did you shoot Barney Crocker?"

"No. I didn't do nothing."

I shot just above his head and plaster rained down on him.

Jimmy shrieked, trying to cower and only then realizing he was firmly tied up. "Wh-what are you? A cop?"

"No," I said.

That scared him, all right. His eyes went wide and watery.

"Did you or did you not shoot Barney Crocker?"

"I didn't."

I shot directly below the first shot. "Every time you lie to me, the shot gets closer to your head."

"This is coercion in the extreme, Chaplin," Gamma said, though she didn't sound disapproving in my ear.

"All right, I did it, OK?" Jimmy cried out. "I did it, but I didn't mean to. I didn't mean to. I just wanted to scare that lady, Lisa, because Mr. Cole said to do that. You know, just fire a shot above her head, but I got distracted."

"Distracted," I said.

"Sure. Distracted. And it was dark too, OK? I missed."

"And hit Barney Crocker."

"Yeah," he said. "I killed Barney by accident. I just wanted to scare Lisa, I swear."

"I appreciate your honesty." Again, I holstered my weapon, removed the pill from my pocket, and fed it to him like he was a dog. He was out like a light within seconds.

I moved to the desk, rewound the tape on the recording device, and deleted my voice from the tape.

"You're running out of time, Chaplin," Gamma breathed in my ear.

I hit play on the tape.

First Mr. Cole's voice came through. *"I hired him to scare the woman, Lisa. That's it. I didn't say nothing about shooting. I didn't say nothing about murder. If he killed him, that's on him."*

And then Jimmy Dolgner's. *"I killed Barney by accident. I just wanted to scare Lisa, I swear."*

"Got it," I said to Gamma. "I'm on my way out."

"You'd better use a back exit. There are police tearing down the road. Sirens and lights."

Kimberly, upon my encouragement, had gone to the police about her boyfriend and what she'd seen.

"Roger that." I exited the office, leaving the door open, and moved through the building until I found a bathroom. I punched out the window then crawled through it, trusting the armor to protect me from glass. "I'm on my way to you," I whispered, my heart lifting.

I had done it. I had found the truth, with a lot of help from my grandmother and my good friend, but it was out there.

Now, all I had to worry about was my impending court case.

# Twenty



"I'm so glad that's the case," Gamma said, turning to me with a glass of wine in hand.

"Apparently, the charges have been miraculously dropped. The prosecutor didn't think the case had enough evidence," I replied. "I wonder how that happened."

"I have no idea what you're insinuating." But my grandmother had a twinkle in her eye.

It was Thanksgiving, and this morning, I had received the best news all week. The charges against me for "Interfering with Public Duties" had been dropped. I wouldn't have to appear in court, I wouldn't have to worry about a hefty fine or jail time, and I would be *exceedingly* careful in future.

Because no way would I stop investigating cases or fixing people's problems in Gossip. If I'd learned anything about myself over the past little while, it was that I belonged here and that I didn't want to leave.

Every time something bad happened, I wanted to get involved. It didn't matter whether there was a paycheck or not. I cared about my grandmother, this town, and the people in it. Most of the people.

Mr. Cole, the loan shark, could take a hike off the end of a short pier as far as I was concerned.

"Is everybody ready?" Lauren asked, emerging from the kitchen's swinging doors with their porthole windows, and out into the dining area.

Gamma and I had set up a long table for all the guests, including Jason, Lauren's husband, and her two children. Quinton had joined us as well, but there was no sign of the special guest that was meant to be joining us.

"She's late," Gamma grumbled. "Of course, she's late. Absolutely typical."

"Who?" I asked.

"You'll see."

"Georgina?" Lauren raised an eyebrow.

"Bring out the turkey, Lauren. We're starving out here," my grandmother said. "I'm sure our guest won't mind us eating when she could hardly bring herself to arrive on time."

A booming knock came at the inn's front doors, and even the cats, all three of them had taken up positions on chairs near the dining room front windows, jolted. They looked kind of adorable, with bow-ties attached to their collars, and empty kitty bowls sitting on the table in front of them, waiting for their share of the thanksgiving turkey —no gravy, of course.

"Ah," Gamma said. "She's here." She rose and exited into the hall.

Everyone at the table exchanged glances. Who could it be, this surprise guest?

I found I didn't care all that much. The relief of having those charges dropped was bone deep. It was what I was truly thankful for this year. Among other things, all of which revolved around the inn, Gossip, and most especially my grandmother and Lauren.

Gamma came around the corner with another woman beside her. A woman with short brown hair, sparkling eyes, and wearing a tartan pashmina.

Jessie Belle-Blue.

Here.

Under the Gossip Inn's roof? With Gamma's permission?

I rose from my chair.

"Easy, Charlotte," Gamma said. "Jessie's joining us under the banner of a truce today. Isn't that right?"

"That's correct, Georgina."

They had called each other by their first names. What was this madness? Gamma could barely stand to breathe the same air as Belle-Blue most days.

"I thought that since it's Thanksgiving and Jessie's husband is away on a business trip, and Quinton doesn't get to see his aunt too much, it might be nice for them to spend family time together," Gamma said. "Please, take a seat. Don't mind the stares. They'll get used to the idea."

"Thank you, Georgina." Belle-Blue sat down next to her nephew.

"Am I... awake right now?" I asked.

Gamma resumed her seat beside me, smiling. "Relax, Charlotte. Things will go straight back to normal tomorrow."

"You can count on that," Belle-Blue said.

But it was quite something to behold. It was testament to the fact that good food and thanks really did bring people together. That or Gamma had actually lost it, and I needed to take her for a CT scan as soon as possible.

"Just because we're at war," Gamma said, "doesn't mean we can't be civilized on important days."

"Sure." I'd withhold my disbelief for now, but Gamma would be getting an earful from me later.

Now, however, it was time to celebrate. I went into the kitchen and helped Lauren bring out the host of amazing food, from the turkey to cranberry sauce, to roast vegetables, mashed potatoes, sweet potato bake complete with pecan topping, and pumpkin pie and pecan pie.

The table groaned under the weight of all the dishes, and by the end of it, I was groaning just as much. I wasn't the only one.

"Now would be a good time to go around the table and say what we're thankful for this year," Gamma said. "I'm thankful for this inn and the family I have right here."

Lauren and I smiled at her.

"I'm thankful for good food," Belle-Blue said.

"For Charlie," Quinton said, in reference to his husky who was under the table, snacking on turkey.

"For my children and husband." That was from Lauren.

"For my wife and children," Jason said, copying Lauren.

"I'm thankful for—"

Another booming knock interrupted me. I rose from the table. "I'll get it," I said. "I need to walk off some of the calories anyway."

The chatter at the table resumed as I headed past the cat's table—they had already finished their turkey and sat in various states of purring joy, afterward—and out into the hall.

I opened the front door and found Detective Goode standing on the doorstep. No lanyard, just a fluffy sweater, a pair of jeans, and an earnest expression on his handsome face.

"Detective Goode," I said. "Happy Thanksgiving."

"I'm sorry."

"What?"

"For arresting you."

"That's your job," I said. "You don't need to be sorry about that."

"Maybe that makes me a bad detective, but I'm still sorry."

"That's... fine. Like I said, it's your job." I hesitated. I liked to dislike Detective Goode a little too much, but it was Thanksgiving. I ought to invite him in for something to eat or drink. "Do you want to—"

"I know it's you who's doing this."

"Huh?"

"Catching criminals. Leaving evidence at the scene," he said. "You're making waves."

"I have no idea what you're talking about." The official party line.

"You don't get it," he said. "I know you're the one

doing it, but I don't care." And then he swept me into his arms, drew me close, and planted a kiss square on my lips.

I nearly melted into a puddle of Charlotte chocolate. The kiss was stunning, a zinger. Warm and sweet, and nothing like I'd ever experienced before. I'd thought I'd kissed my ex-husband, but this was different. It was living.

Finally, he released me, and I stood there, swaying on the spot and unable to conjure up a single snappy thing to say.

"I just wanted you to know that I'm thankful for you this year." And then he jogged back down the steps and toward his car. He was gone within minutes, and I stood there, staring blankly ahead.

A small smile parted my lips. Slowly, I shut the inn's front doors, turned and went to rejoin my friends and family. I knew what I was thankful for this year.

*Charlie and Gamma's adventures continue in* The Case of the Shortcake Serenade, A Gossip Cozy Mystery Book 5.

# Craving More Cozy Mystery?

**If you had fun with Charlie and Gamma, you'll want to meet Milly and her pet bunny Waffle. You can read the first chapter of Milly's story below!**

"It's unheard of! A travesty." My grandmother, Cecelia Pepper, sat on the edge of her seat at the coffee bar in the Starlight Cafe. "Why, the sheriff ought to be ashamed of himself. How are we meant to walk down the streets in this town with this... threat in the backs of our minds? Looming! Like some giant Sword of Damocles over our heads." She tapped the newspaper, a copy of *The Star Lake Gazette*, she'd laid on the coffee bar the minute she'd sat down.

My grandmother was the definition of dynamite in a

small package. At 75-years-old, she was brimming with vigor to make up for her height.

"I'm sure Sheriff Rogers will figure it out." I fixed Gran a cup of coffee—a hazelnut latte with extra cream—and placed it in front of her. "It's a small town, Gran. They'll catch whoever's doing this."

"A small town that's going downhill quickly." My grandmother glanced around as if she was afraid of someone overhearing our conversation.

But the painful truth was there was nobody in my cafe this morning. Just like there'd been nobody in it the day before.

As I'd learned quickly, folks in Star Lake, Iowa, were insular. They didn't care that my late father, a town favorite, had left me the cafe. I hadn't lived in town long enough for them to trust me, and then there was the fact that I had absolutely no experience in the hospitality industry.

*Not now. Just take a breath and smile.*

"I mean, really. A mugger? Here? Nancy from the bakery told me her sister's best friend's cousin was attacked. Wallet stolen. Can you believe that? If I didn't love the lake and the people so much," my grandmother continued, lifting the latte, "I'd move away in a heartbeat."

"Gran."

"I'm serious."

"Gran, you've lived here for thirty-five years."

"Fine. I might not move, but I'll protest this at the next town council meeting. You can mark my words on that." Gran took a sip of her latte, pressed her lips together and fluttered her eyelashes. "Nearly as good as your father used to make."

A silence ensued, filled with our shared sorrow. It was too soon to talk about him.

I cast my gaze away from Gran and studied the interior of the cafe. Light streamed through the windows and the glass front doors, illuminating the linoleum that was in need of a revamp, as well as the checked tablecloths and laminated menus. The chairs were comfortable and well worn. The cash register was an antique and the walls were dark wood.

Overall, the aesthetic was typical of my dad's taste. Hastily thrown together but with plenty of heart.

"This really is good." Gran must've noticed the lump in my throat. Metaphorically, of course. "You know, you'll make a fine restaurant owner. As fine an owner as you would've made a detective."

That was another touchy subject. "Thanks, Gran." I forced a smile.

She reached over and patted my forearm.

Movement outside on the brick-paved sidewalk caught my attention. A homeless woman, wearing a shabby coat and carrying several plastic bags, walked up and took a seat outside the cafe.

"Oh dear," Gran said.

"Do you know her?"

"Only by sight," Gran replied. "She's new to town I think. I'm not familiar with her story. Poor woman."

I bit down on my lip then headed back to the coffee machine and started fixing another latte. Much to my surprise, the bell over the door tinkled, and Sheriff Rogers entered.

He was in his late fifties, with a gray mustache, balding, and wearing his uniform with pride. He sauntered over to the bar and eyed me. "Morning."

"Good morning, Sheriff," I said. "What can I get for you today?"

The sheriff didn't immediately answer me. He scanned the interior of the cafe then pointed over to a new section I'd set up, with the help of my cook, Francesca. "What's that?"

"That's the waffle station," I said, smiling. "Do you want to try it out? We prepare the waffles fresh, bring 'em out to you, and then you decorate them as you see fit. There's ice cream and maple syrup, there's—"

"That wasn't here when Frank was running the place."

"No," I said. "No, it wasn't. I figured that people would enjoy—"

"Waffles?"

"Sheriff Rogers," my grandmother said, and the sheriff jumped a little.

"Celia." He sniffed, using Gran's nickname. "Shoot. I didn't see you there." And he sounded truly regretful, like he was anticipating a volley of complaints. He wouldn't have been wrong in that respect.

"What's this I hear about a mugger?" Gran tapped the newspaper. "A mugger in our midst?"

"Well, yeah, there have been reports of muggings over the past week, but I assure you it's under control."

"Now, Sheriff, you know better than to shovel that level of manure around me," Gran said. "I want answers, and I want them now. What am I supposed to tell the ladies in my book club? That we can't walk to the library in peace?"

"I assure you..."

The conversation faded out as I finished off the latte, grabbed a cupcake from the display of about a dozen under the glass counter, and walked out into the sunlight.

It was the end of summer, the weather a temperate 70 degrees with a soft breeze brushing down the street. I stopped in front of the homeless woman.

"Good morning," I said.

She glared at me, her skin tan, and her ire obvious. "What do you want, Red?"

The urge to brush my fingers through my red hair nearly overtook me. Thankfully, my hands were full. "Uh."

"Let me guess. You want me to move. It's a free country, you know, I—"

"No," I said. "I just wanted to check if you were OK."

"OK?"

"Yeah." I handed her the coffee and the cupcake. "You need anything?" It was my experience, after working as a beat cop in the city, that everyone had a story. Just like everyone had a purpose. Sometimes life just... got in the way.

The woman blinked. "Uh. Yeah. I'm good. Thanks."

"Sure. Just holler if you need a glass of water or something," I said. "I'll be inside."

The woman, still full of mistrust, nodded then took a sip of her coffee. I headed back into the cafe and found Gran and Sheriff Rogers embroiled in their argument.

"—muggers on the streets. If you think that we'll stand for this then you're delusional. You know, I can call up the heads of the three factions, right now, and get them to arrange a meeting."

Sheriff Rogers, blustery as he was, paled at that.

The "factions" as they were called, were the three unions that pretty much ran Star Lake. There were "the boaters", "the butchers", and "the bakers"—and they frequently disagreed on issues, to the point where the town was practically split into three. It was expected that you'd fall into line with one of the groups even if you weren't an active member of said union.

"The bakers would be most interested to hear about your lack of action when it comes to crime on our streets. I mean, this whole area is packed with bakeries and restaurants. This is bound to affect tourism too. And then the boaters will get antsy."

The summer months in Star Lake were famed for their fun boating activities, from tours on the lake, to fishing, to jet skiing and recreational activities.

"You're complaining about mugging and crime on the street," Sheriff Rogers said, finding his voice, "yet you won't stop your granddaughter over here from feeding said criminals."

Gran jerked back as if she'd been slapped—a strange effect on a tiny woman in a floral-print dress. "Feeding them? I think the heat is getting to you, Sheriff."

"She just took out a coffee and a cupcake to…" He trailed off and gestured toward the homeless woman now sitting on a bench out front.

"And so?" Gran grew red and rose from her barstool, trying to tower at four feet eight inches.

The sheriff tugged on his collar. "All I'm saying is that if you don't want trouble, don't invite it into your home."

And with that, he swept from the cafe, trailing his overbearing spicy cologne.

"Idiot," Gran muttered.

"Gran."

"There's no love lost between us." She resumed her seat. "And for good reason."

But she didn't go into the reason. I fixed a cup of coffee for Francesca, who was in the kitchen, patiently awaiting orders that would likely never come, and then joined my grandmother at the counter.

Gran paged through the newspaper, stopping on an image and tapping it. "See, now, this is why you don't want to get on the wrong side of those boaters. Look at that. A full page ad for their 'Boating Blowout 2021.'"

I read over her shoulder. "Join us for a boating extravaganza as we celebrate the end of summer."

"You're going, I assume? Everyone's going," Gran said. "Everybody who's anybody. It will be a great opportunity for you to network, dear. It's been a year, and you've only made one friend."

"Thanks, Gran."

"I'm just saying," she replied, "that it might be a good opportunity for you to get out there and meet someone."

"Meet someone? The only person I'm interested in meeting is an accountant who can help me manage my finances for this place." Things were *not* looking good.

And I was *not* about to let down my father's legacy by losing the Starlight Cafe.

"I'm sure there are plenty of eligible accountants around."

"Not what I meant, Gran."

She gave me a sneaky smile, and it cheered me up. I couldn't stay mad at Gran.

"Are you coming by tonight for supper?" Gran asked. "I'm making chicken casserole. You can bring Waffle along."

"That sounds great."

It sure beat eating a microwave dinner over the kitchen sink.

Want to read more? You can grab **the first book on all major retailers.**

Happy reading, friend!

Paperbacks Available by Rosie A. Point

*A Burger Bar Mystery series*

*The Fiesta Burger Murder*

*The Double Cheese Burger Murder*

*The Chicken Burger Murder*

*The Breakfast Burger Murder*

*The Salmon Burger Murder*

*The Cheesy Steak Burger Murder*

*A Bite-sized Bakery Cozy Mystery series*

*Murder by Chocolate*

*Marzipan and Murder*

*Creepy Cake Murder*

*Murder and Meringue Cake*

*Murder Under the Mistletoe*

*Murder Glazed Donuts*

*Choc Chip Murder*

*Macarons and Murder*

*Candy Cake Murder*

*Murder by Rainbow Cake*

<u>*A Milly Pepper Mystery series*</u>

*Maple Drizzle Murder*


<u>*A Sunny Side Up Cozy Mystery series*</u>

*Murder Over Easy*

*Muffin But Murder*

*Chicken Murder Soup*

*Murderoni and Cheese*

*Lemon Murder Pie*


<u>*A Gossip Cozy Mystery series*</u>

*The Case of the Waffling Warrants*


<u>*A Mission Inn-possible Cozy Mystery series*</u>

*Vanilla Vendetta*

*Strawberry Sin*

*Cocoa Conviction*

*Mint Murder*

*Raspberry Revenge*

*Chocolate Chills*


<u>*A Very Murder Christmas series*</u>

*Dachshund Through the Snow*

*Owl Be Home for Christmas*